TEDDY JO

and the Strange Medallion

TEDDY JO

AND THE
Strange Medallion

HILDA STAHL

 BOOKS

Tyndale House Publishers, Inc., Wheaton, Illinois

Dedicated with love to Diane and Elias Torres

Teddy Jo Series
 1 Teddy Jo and the Terrible Secret
 2 Teddy Jo and the Yellow Room Mystery
 3 Teddy Jo and the Stolen Ring
 4 Teddy Jo and the Strangers in the Pink House
 5 Teddy Jo and the Strange Medallion
 6 Teddy Jo and the Wild Dog
 7 Teddy Jo and the Abandoned House
 8 Teddy Jo and the Ragged Beggars
 9 Teddy Jo and the Kidnapped Heir
10 Teddy Jo and the Great Dive
11 Teddy Jo and the Magic Quill
12 Teddy Jo and the Broken Locket Mystery
13 Teddy Jo and the Missing Portrait
14 Teddy Jo and the Missing Family

Cover illustration by Gail Owens

Juvenile trade paper edition

Library of Congress Catalog Card Number 89-50616
ISBN 0-8423-6977-5
Copyright 1983 by Hilda Stahl
All rights reserved
Printed in the United States of America

1 2 3 4 5 6 7 8 9 10 95 94 93 92 91 90 89

Contents

1   Help in the Storm   9

2   Grace Guthrie   17

3   The $100 Bill   27

4   The $100 Returned   35

5   Mean Marsha   43

6   Marsha's Secret   53

7   The Medallion   63

8   Snowdrifts   73

9   Christmas   83

10   Marsha to the Rescue   91

11   The Bagpipe   99

12   New Clothes   105

13   A Family Reunited   113

14   Easter   121

1. Help
in the Storm

The strong November wind whipped Teddy
Jo's dark hair as she raced angrily after Marsha
Wyman. "Give back my soccer ball, Marsha!"
The wind caught the sharp words and carried
them back so that Paul heard them as he
struggled to catch up to Teddy Jo.

Marsha clutched the red and white soccer
ball tighter and giggled as she ran faster. Teddy
Jo and her little brother would never get the
ball back! Marsha's cheeks were as red as her
long hair. Her blue winter jacket blocked
out most of the cold air. Her jeans were tucked
into her high winter boots with the white fur
around the top. She was going to make Teddy
Jo sorry that her family had moved to Middle
Lake!

Teddy Jo's lungs ached. She wanted to sprint
faster and grab Marsha around the legs and
tumble her to the frozen ground, but she knew

Paul was trying to keep up with her. She couldn't leave him too far behind or he'd get scared, and if he got scared he'd wet his pants and that would be a million times worse than letting Marsha get away with her soccer ball. Marsha had to go home sometime and since they lived across the street from each other, she'd get her ball back one way or another. She pressed her lips tightly together and narrowed her blue eyes. She'd get her soccer ball back all right.

The houses on this part of Lincoln Street were old and run-down. No kids were playing in the yards or on the street. Paul knew they were probably all inside watching Saturday cartoons, the same as he would be doing now if Marsha hadn't taken the soccer ball while they were playing in the park. He had told Teddy Jo that it was too windy and cold to play in the park, but she'd dragged him out of the house and away from the TV. Once he got big, he'd never let her do that again. He'd watch cartoons all his life if he wanted to. Teddy Jo could just play soccer alone. Ever since she got a soccer ball for her eleventh birthday in July, she thought she was hot stuff. Someday he'd own ten soccer balls if he wanted and he'd line them all up in his room and show them off to Teddy Jo. A sharp pain stabbed his side and he doubled over, stumbled, then ran on.

Marsha looked over her shoulder and

laughed wickedly. She stubbed her toe on a crack and staggered forward. Abruptly she flung out her arms to catch her balance and the ball rolled across a yard and bumped against a wooden step that led up to a lavender house. She gasped, and her heart raced in alarm. Was she that far down Lincoln Street? Oh, what had she been thinking of? She had to get away from here now! She glanced back to find Teddy Jo too close for comfort. She'd have to leave the ball or be caught. With a wild look around, she ran down the sidewalk, then ducked behind an old brown station wagon falling apart with rust. Her lungs ached and the wind whistled around her, blowing dust and old papers along the gutter. She shivered and hunched her thin shoulders.

Teddy Jo hesitated, her thin chest rising and falling. She wanted to grab her ball and run home, but she wanted to get Marsha, too.

Paul finally caught up to her, gasping for breath. He dropped to the frozen ground and sucked in great gulps of air. His lips were blue from the cold and his fingers felt stiff inside his brown mittens. Would Teddy Jo grab her ball and then chase after Marsha? Oh, he hoped not! He wanted to go home where it was warm. He'd make himself a peanut butter and mustard sandwich, get a glass of Pepsi, and watch TV the rest of the day.

Teddy Jo scooped up her red and white ball and hugged it to her as she looked around through narrowed eyes for mean Marsha Wyman. How dare Marsha touch her ball! Did she put any scratches on it? Teddy Jo turned it in her hands, inspecting it with great care. This was her ball, her very own soccer ball that friends had given her for her birthday, and she wanted to keep it forever.

"Where did Marsha go?" she asked between clenched teeth. She looked around, but the only person she could see was a small old lady struggling against the wind with a bag of groceries clutched in her arms. It was the old woman, Grace Guthrie, that everyone made fun of.

Marsha saw the old woman and panic seized her. What if Grace Guthrie saw her? She shrank closer to the tire of the station wagon. The bag lady walked closer, fighting against the strong wind, her old coat flapping around her thin legs that were covered with worn black slacks. Everyone called her the bag lady because she walked around Middle Lake carrying a bag in each arm. She picked up everything that she felt would be of value to her. She bought groceries with the money she was given for the pop cans and bottles. She saved lost gloves and every bit of string that she found. Someone said that her house was full of things that she saved, even the containers that Big Macs came in. It would be terrible if Grace Guthrie saw her! Marsha turned her face away and waited without breathing until she was sure the old woman was past the station wagon.

Teddy Jo saw the old woman's battered black hat sail from her head and fly into the street. "Wait here, Paul." She pushed her ball into his arms and ran down the sidewalk. She didn't want to speak to the old woman or be near her, but Teddy Jo couldn't let the wind steal the old lady's hat and freeze her ears.

Grace Guthrie stopped and dropped her bag, but before she could make a move to get her hat, Teddy Jo picked it up and ran back with it.

"Give me my hat, little girl!" cried the old woman with a catch in her rough voice. She reached out to grab it and her angle twisted and she started to fall. She cried out in alarm as she grabbed Teddy Jo's thin arm.

Teddy Jo gripped the woman's hand and fell with her, but managed to break her fall. "Are you all right?" Teddy Jo saw tears in the faded blue eyes and she was surprised. She didn't think bag ladies cried. The wind ruffled the thin gray hair. Her face was lined with deep wrinkles and she smelled as if she hadn't taken a bath in a long time.

"I think I'm all right, little girl." Grace tugged her hat over her head and down over her ears, then struggled until she finally stood on her feet. She wore ragged tennis shoes much too large for her. She tried first one foot and then the other, clinging to Teddy Jo's shoulder. Finally she nodded. "Sure enough, little girl. I'm right as rain. Oh, but my groceries are spread all around!"

"I'll get them." Teddy Jo stuck the cans of vegetables and a box of saltines in the bag. "I'll carry it. If I'm careful the sack won't rip any more and nothing will fall out."

"You don't have to help me. I can manage on my own."

"I don't mind. Where do you live?"

Grace sighed and pointed up ahead. "In that lavender house. What's that little boy doing in my yard? He'd better not be stealing anything of mine!"

"No, it's all right," said Teddy Jo quickly. "That's my brother, Paul. He's waiting for me. I saw the wind blow your hat off and I told him to wait for me while I helped you."

Grace looked at her sharply. "Can I trust you?"

"Yes."

"I can't trust some, you know."

"You can trust me. Honest."

"Then I'll let you help me. But don't expect no pay! I'm a poor old lady." She drooped her thin shoulders even more and let her mouth sag a little.

Teddy Jo bit the inside of her bottom lip. She could suddenly tell that Grace Guthrie was exaggerating just as Teddy Jo did when she wanted to have her own way or when she wanted someone to feel sorry for her. She stopped outside the door and the wind howled louder and blew stronger. "I'm not doing this for pay. I only want to help."

Grace pursed her lips, then finally unlocked the heavy front door and pushed it open. "Set down my bag and be on your way."

The stuffiness choked Teddy Jo as she stepped around a pile of cardboard boxes. Smells of old papers and cooked onions hung in the air. Teddy Jo set the bag on the only chair that wasn't piled high with stuff, said good-bye stiffly, and walked out, glad for the fresh air.

Paul ran to her, the ball firmly in his arms. "What happened, Teddy Jo? Did she try to lock you in and keep you?"

Teddy Jo frowned at Paul. "Of course not! She's only an old woman, not a wicked witch or anything."

Paul sighed in relief, then turned with Teddy Jo toward home.

The door to the lavender house opened and Grace Guthrie called in a scratchy voice, "Wait, little girl! Wait! Don't take another step!"

Teddy Jo froze, her blue eyes wide with sudden fear.

2. Grace Guthrie

"Did you want me, Mrs. Guthrie?" asked Teddy Jo in a shaky voice.

Paul crept close to Teddy Jo and watched as the old woman shuffled toward them in her large tennis shoes that were tied with brown laces. He wanted to pull Teddy Jo away from the lavender house and run home with her. His stomach cramped and a shiver ran down his spine.

Marsha peeked around the station wagon with a frown. Why didn't the wind stop blowing so she could hear what they were saying? What if Grace Guthrie told Teddy Jo the terrible truth? Oh, but Teddy Jo would love to spread the awful story all around Middle Lake!

Grace stopped just inches from Teddy Jo. "Where is it, little girl?" Her face was dark with anger. "You said I could trust you!"

Teddy Jo stumbled back. She wanted to turn and run, but she stood her ground. "What do you think I did?"

"You took my medallion!"

"No!" Teddy Jo shook her head. Her face was freezing and the end of her nose felt as if it would break off.

"We don't even know what a medallion is," shouted Paul over the wind. Grace turned her watery blue eyes on him and he pulled into himself and snapped his mouth closed in fear.

"It's a funny-looking necklace about this big." Grace made an oval shape with her finger and thumb. "And it hangs on a heavy gold chain."

"I didn't see it." Teddy Jo shook her head again. Oh, why had she bothered helping the cranky old lady? "I don't steal." And she didn't either. She hadn't even before she had learned about Jesus and had asked him into her life. She had lied and sworn and had had temper tantrums and flown into rages and hit anyone in sight, but she had never stolen anything. "Paul and me are going home now. We don't know anything about your funny necklace."

"Medallion."

"Medallion." Teddy Jo turned to leave, but Grace wrapped her clawlike fingers around her arm just above her wrist. Teddy Jo lifted startled eyes, then relaxed when she saw the tears in the old woman's eyes.

"I've got to have my medallion. I've got to!

I had it on around my neck where I always wear it and now it's gone! It was there when I left the grocery store."

"Maybe you dropped it when you fell. The chain maybe broke."

Paul moved restlessly from one booted foot to the other. He had to go to the bathroom and he couldn't wait much longer. He didn't dare say anything or the old woman might look at him again and scare him.

Teddy Jo hesitated. They really should get home, but Mrs. Guthrie did need help. "Me and Paul will go look for it."

"Not on your life! I'll keep the boy here with me while you go. Then you won't run off if you find it." Grace gripped Paul's sleeve and he was too frightened to move.

Teddy Jo saw the pinched look around Paul's mouth and she knew he was afraid. She had to do something to help him before he wet his pants and embarrassed them both. She swallowed hard. "You let Paul go inside and use your bathroom and I'll be back in a flash."

Paul blushed as he stared down at the wide crack in the sidewalk. He sure should've stayed home this morning.

"Me and the boy will wait inside out of the cold. But you'd better come right back, little girl!" Grace bobbed her head up and down. "I mean it!"

"You'd better," muttered Paul with a dark scowl. Someday he'd be so brave that he wouldn't let an old lady and an eleven-year-old sister order him around.

Teddy Jo turned abruptly away and ran against the cold, strong wind. Her eyes watered. Long brown hair whipped against her face, stinging her cheeks. Why, oh, why had she helped Grace Guthrie in the first place? Everyone knew how mean she was. What if Paul wasn't safe being with her?

Teddy Jo's heart beat faster and she looked back over her shoulder. No one stood in front of the lavender house. All the houses looked deserted, but she knew people lived inside, people who wouldn't bother helping others.

She stopped at the spot where Grace had fallen and she bent down and looked around. Her legs felt frozen against her jeans. Even with warm winter boots her toes ached with cold. She found an orange button, several pull tabs off pop cans and a Milky Way candy wrapper. Impatiently she kicked a pile of brown leaves caught against a short fence. The leaves scattered. The wind caught a few and whirled them farther down the street. Teddy Jo sighed, then leaned forward, her eyes wide. A heavy gold chain peeked out of the leaves. She muffled a glad cry as she lifted the chain and the strange medallion. It dangled from her hand, swinging back and forth. She smiled. With a whoop of joy she ran toward the lavender house with the medallion firmly in her hand.

Marsha frowned from behind the station wagon. Her back ached and she wanted to stand, but she didn't dare take a chance that Teddy Jo would see her. What had Teddy Jo picked up? Why was she running back to the lavender house? Marsha closed her eyes and groaned. Was her whole life going to be ruined because of Teddy Jo Miller?

Teddy Jo knocked on the lavender door and immediately it swung open. "I found it!" she said with a happy smile that made her blue eyes sparkle.

"Don't just stand there! Come in! I don't pay to heat the whole outdoors, you know." Grace jerked Teddy Jo inside so hard she almost fell. "Now, where is it?"

"Here."

Grace caught the medallion to her and her face crumpled and tears ran down her wrinkled cheeks.

Teddy Jo looked away, flushed with embarrassment. Where was Paul? They should leave now. Had Mrs. Guthrie done something terrible to Paul? Why hadn't he come running when he heard her knock?

Grace hung the medallion around her neck and it settled in place on the heavy black sweater she wore. She pulled a tissue from her sleeve and wiped her tears and noisily blew her nose. "Come to the kitchen with me. I want to give you something."

Teddy Jo started to object, but already Grace

was marching away down the narrow path toward the back of the house.

Paul looked up from the table that stood in the middle of the crowded kitchen. He rubbed the milk off his mouth with the back of his hand and swallowed the bite of cookie. "Did you find it?"

"Yes." Teddy Jo frowned at him. He knew better than to sit and eat at a stranger's table.

Paul ducked his head and took another bite of the round chocolate cookie that Mrs. Guthrie had said she'd made early this morning. The cookie was delicious and he sure wouldn't quit eating it just because Teddy Jo was frowning at him.

"Sit down and have cookies and milk with us." Grace pulled out a padded dinette chair and pushed Teddy Jo down into it.

"We can't stay."

"I won't let you leave without giving you something for your trouble. Grace Guthrie don't take charity! I pay my own way in this world!"

Teddy Jo squirmed restlessly. "Maybe I should call home and tell them we'll be late for lunch." The big clock over the refrigerator said twelve already. "Grandpa is coming for lunch and he's planning on seeing us."

"Who's your grandpa?"

"Ed Korman."

Grace stopped with a glass of milk in her

hand. "I know him. He lives right outside of town and has all them black walnut trees. Sure, I know him."

"He's our grandpa," said Paul.

"He has a daughter. You must be her kids."

Teddy Jo nodded and gladly took the glass of milk. They were strangers no longer; Grace Guthrie knew Grandpa. "This is Paul, and I'm Teddy Jo Miller."

"Teddy Jo? Strange name for a girl."

She gulped down half the milk. "It's short for Theodora Josephine."

"I can see why you settle for Teddy Jo." Grace sat down across from Paul and Teddy Jo. "Do you live right here in town?"

"Just a few blocks away. 712 Oak Street."

Grace gasped and the color drained from her face. "I thought Cooks lived there." Her voice came out in a higher pitch and Teddy Jo looked at her strangely.

"We moved in last year." Teddy Jo dropped the cookie back on the plate and locked her trembling hands in her lap.

Grace rubbed her wrinkled hand across her eyes. "Don't let me worry you none, Teddy Jo. An old lady gets crazy notions sometimes." She leaned forward and the medallion bumped against the table. She lovingly cupped it in her hand. "I'm glad to have this back. I wouldn't have slept well tonight without it."

"What's so special about it?" asked Paul, his

boots dangling several inches from the linoleum-covered floor. His feet were hot inside his boots.

Grace rubbed a finger across the face of the medallion, then held it out. "This came from Scotland many years ago. It was passed down through my husband's family and when he went to his reward five years ago, it came to me."

"That's sure a funny-looking lady." Paul wrinkled his small nose.

"It's a Scotsman in a kilt, playing the pipes." Grace smiled as her eyes misted with tears. "I had me a son and he learned the bagpipe, but he died when he was in high school. My daughter took the bagpipe and hid it away in the attic in her house. She won't let me touch it or see it." Grace sniffed loudly, then tossed her head. "Enough of that! I won't talk about the daughter that I don't have!"

Teddy Jo glanced at the clock. "Mrs. Guthrie, I should call home. Could I use your phone, please?"

"It's on the wall beside the back door. I should have it taken out so I don't have to pay them bills, but I just never get around to it."

Teddy Jo quickly dialed her number, then waited, standing on first one foot and then the other. Finally her dad answered. She swallowed hard. "Dad, it's Teddy Jo. Me and Paul are on Lincoln Street, but we'll be home as soon as we can."

"What in the world are you doing there? You went to the park."

Teddy Jo squirmed restlessly. "We helped Mrs. Guthrie and we're at her house now. Me and Paul are."

"You're at old Mrs. Guthrie's house?" Larry sounded surprised and impatient and Teddy Jo wished that she hadn't called. "Did you look outside lately? It's snowing and blowing real bad out."

"We'll be careful. We'll be home as soon as we can."

"Just wait there. I'll pick you up. You kids can't be out in this storm." He banged the receiver and Teddy Jo slowly hung up and turned in surprise to Paul.

"Dad's going to pick us up."

Paul's mouth dropped open.

"He is, Paul. So, we'd better watch for him so we can run right out to the car when he comes." Teddy Jo dropped back on the chair, shaking her head. Dad had never done anything this nice before. Was he changing like Grandpa had said he would? Would the whole family be Christians someday? She and Paul and Mom were, but not Dad or Linda. But Grandpa had said that he was praying for all of them, and he said God would answer.

"I have something for you," said Grace as she reached up in a tall cluttered cupboard. "Grace Guthrie always pays her own way."

"I don't need pay." Teddy Jo reluctantly

held out her hand and Grace pushed a folded bill into it. "I really don't want this."

"Stuff it in your pocket and hush up! Grace Guthrie always pays her own way!"

Teddy Jo pushed the money into her jeans and motioned to Paul. "Thanks for the cookies and milk, Mrs. Guthrie. We'd better go now."

Paul picked up the soccer ball and followed Teddy Jo to the door. He wanted Mrs. Guthrie to push money into his hand, too, but he pressed his lips tightly together and didn't say anything. Teddy Jo would close his mouth for him if he asked for money.

Dust drifted down from the faded curtain as Teddy Jo pushed it aside to look outdoors. Snow swirled around, making it almost impossible to see. Would Dad be mad because he had to come get them? Her stomach tightened. Would he ever get mad enough to walk out on them again, as he had when she was ten and Paul six? Oh, she couldn't think about that!

"There's a car now," said Grace in her gruff voice. "Good-bye, Teddy Jo. Good-bye, Paul."

"Bye." Teddy Jo opened the door and stepped out into the freezing, swirling storm.

3. The $100 Bill

Teddy Jo huddled in the corner of the warm
car, thankful to be out of the cold. Paul sat
beside her, hunched into himself, his little face
white and scared. She wanted to lean over
and whisper to him that Dad didn't look angry,
but she didn't dare, or for sure he would get
angry. She swallowed hard. "Dad, thanks for
picking us up. It would've been terrible
walking."

"Yes, well, you're just lucky you were able
to get to a phone." He turned onto Oak Street.
"What were you doing so far from Greer Park?"

"Marsha took Teddy Jo's soccer ball!" Paul
leaned forward against the seat. "We almost
caught her, but she dropped the ball and then
Mrs. Guthrie came along and dropped her
groceries. She bakes good cookies."

Teddy Jo locked her fingers together and
waited with her breath held. Paul should know

27

to keep his mouth closed! But Dad didn't snap
or swear. Maybe he'd like to see the money
Grace Guthrie had given her. Teddy Jo pulled
out the folded bill. "She gave me money for
helping her, Dad."

"That was nice of her." Larry parked the car
in the garage and looked back at Teddy Jo. "I
don't know how she could afford to. Everyone
knows how poor she is."

"See. Here's the money." Teddy Jo unfolded
it, then stared down at it with wide blue eyes.
She swallowed hard and shot a look at Dad.
"It's not a dollar." Her voice was a husky
whisper and she cleared her throat.

"It's a one hundred dollar bill!" Larry
whistled as he took the bill and studied it in
surprise. "And it's real."

"You're rich, Teddy Jo!" cried Paul. Oh, why
hadn't he asked for a reward even if Teddy Jo
would've socked him!

"I have to take it back! She probably thought
she gave me a dollar. Dad, take me back and
let me return it." Teddy Jo once again held
the money in her hands and stared down at it.
Oh, but it would be great to keep it, but she
just couldn't. Could she?

"She gave it to you." Larry opened the door
and got out. "Let's get into the house before
we freeze!"

Teddy Jo stumbled out and Paul followed
her. "Dad, I can't keep the money!"

"Keep it!" Larry frowned at her. "It was her

28

mistake. If you don't want it, I can sure use it!" He walked into the warm kitchen. Smells of coffee and spaghetti sauce filled the room.

"Teddy Jo got a hundred dollars!" cried Paul as he peeled off his heavy winter coat.

Carol looked up from the kitchen table where she was reading. "Who's kidding who?"

"It's not a joke, Carol." Larry laughed and shook his head. He had dark hair that touched his collar and blue eyes that usually looked sad or frightened.

Carol pushed herself up and tugged her pink sweater down over her jeans. Her dark brown hair curled prettily around her face and her blue eyes were full of questions. "What's this all about?"

Slowly Teddy Jo held out the money and Carol took it. Teddy Jo turned away and hung up her jacket and pulled off her boots. Her toes tingled. She plucked at the sleeves of her navy blue sweat shirt, then tucked her tangled dark hair behind her small ears. Mom would know she couldn't keep the money, wouldn't she? Mom had to understand!

Just then Linda walked in, smelling of perfume. She looked older than thirteen years with heavy makeup on and Carol's flowered blouse tucked into red dress slacks. Her long dark hair hung almost to her narrow waist. "What's this about a hundred dollars?"

Teddy Jo stood quietly beside the kitchen sink while the others looked at the money and talked about Grace Guthrie. Paul liked the attention he was getting and he talked about Mrs. Guthrie and her house. Teddy Jo scowled at him, but he just kept talking. Finally she pulled the money out of Linda's fingers and stuffed it deep into her pocket. "I thought Grandpa was coming for dinner. I'm hungry!"

"He's picking up Anna Sloan." Carol stirred the sauce and meatballs.

Teddy Jo groaned. Now she wouldn't have a minute alone with Grandpa. He sometimes acted as if he liked Anna better than he did her. Would he stop loving her just because of Anna Sloan? Maybe he would marry Anna and tell Teddy Jo to stay away from his house and his animals. Her stomach tightened and her white teeth sank into her pink bottom lip to stop the trembling.

Teddy Jo remembered when she was ten and Mom had forced her to stay with Grandpa. She'd hated him then. She'd hated everyone, especially herself. But Grandpa had loved her and helped her, and finally she had learned to love him. She'd learned that God loved her and wanted to be her heavenly Father. Slowly Teddy Jo's life had changed until she no longer had temper tantrums. She was practically perfect now. She was so nice that it didn't hurt at all to think of returning the money to Mrs. Guthrie. Teddy Jo smiled as she looked out the window. Did her family know just how nice she was? Any time now they'd say, "Isn't Teddy

Jo nice? Why, she's the nicest girl in the whole world!"

The back door opened and Grandpa stood there with Anna Sloan. They were covered with snow and looked cold.

"Grandpa!" cried Teddy Jo happily. She started toward him, then stopped dead. He hadn't even heard her! He didn't even know she was in the kitchen. He was too busy helping Anna off with her coat and asking her if she was warm now. And Anna beamed up at him as if he were the only man in the whole world. Teddy Jo pushed her hands deep into her pockets and hunched her thin shoulders. She touched the folded bill. She'd just keep the money whether Grandpa said to return it or not! That money could buy lots of things. Maybe even a puppy! Wouldn't Paul love that? And if Grandpa said anything at all about the money, she'd just turn away from him and cover her ears with her hands!

Grandpa hiked up his pants and walked across the kitchen. He seemed to fill the room. He wore dark green twill pants and a shirt that he'd bought at Sears in Grand Rapids. Only on Sundays did he wear a white shirt and a suit. He touched Teddy Jo's shoulder and she jerked away from him, her bottom lip stuck out in a pout. The others were talking and laughing with Anna Sloan.

"How's my girl?" asked Grandpa in a low voice for Teddy Jo's ears alone.

She shrugged. Let him go talk to Anna Sloan! Let him go call *her* "his girl"!

"That was very nice of you to help Grace Guthrie."

Teddy Jo lifted her head and looked right into his hazel eyes. "She paid me plenty for it," she snapped. Then she saw the sad, hurt look on Grandpa's face and Teddy Jo turned away before she flung herself into his arms.

Grandpa leaned down with his mouth against her ear. "I love you, Teddy Bear Jo."

Tears filled her eyes and slipped down her cheeks. Finally she turned, and he gathered her close and held her against his heart. He smelled like peppermint and cold air and his own special scent. He caught her hand in his large one and walked her to the living room and sat on the couch with her.

"All right, Teddy Jo. Tell me all about your morning." He brushed her hair back with his work-roughened hand. "Let me see that hundred dollar bill that has everyone so excited."

Slowly she pulled it from her pocket and held it out to him. She told him about Marsha Wyman and about Grace Guthrie and even about her surprise that Dad had picked them up to bring them home so they wouldn't have to walk in the storm.

Grandpa handed back the money and she returned it to her pocket. "You've been busy, Teddy Jo. That was very nice of you to help

32

Mrs. Guthrie. She doesn't have any friends. I think everyone is afraid of her because she's so different. She's lived here for a good five years, I'd say. I don't know if she has family."

"She said she had a son and he died, and she has a daughter but they never see each other."

"What a sad, lonely life she must lead."

"I'm going to take the money back to her, Grandpa."

"I'm glad. I'll drive you over after dinner if you want."

Teddy Jo grinned sheepishly as she thought of her sharp words before. "I'd like that." She rubbed the back of his large hand. "I'm sorry for being bad, Grandpa."

He laughed and hugged her hard. "You're not bad, Teddy Jo. You are very special. Sometimes we all act wrong or do things that we shouldn't. We can ask God to forgive us and then try to do better from then on." He stood up and pulled her up with him. "Right now, we'd better go eat. I hear your mother calling us."

"I'm glad you came today."

"Thanks, honey. I'm glad, too. Anna almost had to stay home to work on her book, but she finally agreed to join us."

Teddy Jo stopped and looked up at Grandpa. "You like Anna a lot, don't you?"

"A whole lot."

"Oh." Teddy Jo began to walk away. A large

hand wrapped around her arm and once again she stopped.

"I have enough love for Anna and you and Paul and all the family, Teddy Jo. I will always love you. You're my Teddy Bear Jo."

A wide smile spread across her face and she practically floated to the table for dinner.

4. The $100 Returned

Teddy Jo knocked on the lavender door. The wind had stopped and only a few flakes fell from the gray sky. Loud music came from the house next door. Teddy Jo looked toward the car where Grandpa and Anna waited for her. They were talking to each other and for just a minute jealousy seized her. She frowned and pushed the terrible feeling away. Grandpa loved her! She didn't need to be jealous of Anna Sloan or anyone else, not even Paul when he climbed on Grandpa's lap and laid his head against Grandpa's broad chest.

Again Teddy Jo knocked. The door burst open and Grace Guthrie glared at Teddy Jo, then gripped her hand and jerked her into the house. Grace slammed the door and stood before Teddy Jo with her fists on her hips and a black look of anger on her face. Teddy Jo swallowed hard and backed against a pile of boxes. A mouse squeeked and scurried out of sight in the rubble.

"I knew I couldn't trust you, Teddy Jo Miller!"

"But you can!"

"No! No, I can't! Any little girl that would come into an old lady's house and steal her blind can't be trusted!" Grace advanced, and Teddy Jo shrank back. "You found my money! You stole it, or that little brother of yours did while my back was turned. I fed you cookies and milk. I let you walk in my house. You touched my medallion!"

Teddy Jo's hand trembled as she reached in her pocket for the folded money. Her voice shook as she said, "I came to return the money you gave me. I didn't want you to pay me for helping you."

Grace shrugged her thin shoulders and tossed her gray head. "Who needs that soiled dollar bill?"

Teddy Jo squared her shoulders and lifted her chin high. "Look at the money, Mrs. Guthrie! Just look at it!"

Grace jerked the bill open, then gasped. She was quiet a long time. Finally, she lifted her head and tears sparkled in her eyes. "I am truly sorry, Teddy Jo. Truly sorry. You were good to me and I snapped at you. I'm sure you'll never forgive me or want to come see me again."

"I can forgive you, Mrs. Guthrie. I do forgive you."

Grace blinked in surprise. "Forgiving is not easy for me."

"Grandpa says that God wants us to forgive, so I do."

Grace dabbed tears from her eyes. "You listen to your grandpa. He makes sense."

"I'd better go now. He's in the car waiting for me."

"Can you come see me again soon?"

Teddy Jo hesitated. Did she really want to come visit in this smelly old house crammed with junk? The lonely look on Grace Guthrie's face decided her. "I'll come. Paul and I will after school sometime."

"I hope you do. I hope you do." Grace fingered the medallion around her neck. Finally she lifted it off over her head. "I want you to have this, Teddy Jo."

"Oh, no! No! You love that! I couldn't take it. You keep it. I will come visit you without any gifts. Honest."

"Well, all right." Grace slipped the heavy chain back over her head and the medallion fell into place on her bulky sweater. "But I'll make cookies for sure."

Teddy Jo smiled. "Thanks. I'll see you another day."

Grace held the door open and Teddy Jo walked out. She ran to the car and turned to wave. Grace Guthrie waved back and finally closed the door. Teddy Jo slipped into the backseat of Grandpa's car.

"So that's Grace Guthrie," said Anna thoughtfully. "I've seen her around town."

"Was she glad to get the money back?" asked Grandpa.

"Yes." If Anna hadn't been sitting in the front seat beside Grandpa, Teddy Jo would've told him just how glad.

She huddled in the far corner and watched as Grandpa drove down the street. She wanted to cover her ears as Grandpa and Anna talked, but she sat with her hands locked in her lap. Maybe Grandpa would drop Anna off and take her home with him. But he dropped her off, said he'd see her Sunday morning, and drove away with Anna.

Teddy Jo stood on the sidewalk outside her house and watched until Grandpa's car was out of sight. Grandpa was spending entirely too much time with Anna Sloan. A dog barked and a pickup drove past. Piano music came from the Brents' house, and Teddy Jo knew Mike was practicing. A movement from across the street caught her attention and she looked at the Wyman house with a frown. Marsha stood in the window and looked back at Teddy Jo. Abruptly Teddy Jo turned and ran to her front door and rushed inside. Dad sat on the couch watching TV. He turned with a frown.

"I'm back," said Teddy Jo weakly as she

pulled off her jacket. She hung it in the hall closet beside Linda's windbreaker.

Larry clicked off the TV and stood with his hands on his lean hips. He was short and slight, and seemed even shorter in his stocking feet. "And did she tell you to keep the money? Did she laugh in your face for being such a jerk?"

Teddy Jo flushed. "She was glad to get it back, Dad. She thought she gave me a dollar. She needed it."

"I'll bet. She probably has money stashed away all over her house. Why should she miss a hundred dollar bill?"

"I couldn't keep it, Dad," Teddy Jo said barely above a whisper.

"Before you got to know Ed Korman you would've kept it! You were a regular pistol, Teddy Jo, but you had lots of smarts. Now, I don't know about you. What kid in her right mind would return easy money like that?"

"I had to, Dad."

He frowned and swore. "Go to your room out of my sight!" He waved his hand and she ran before he got even angrier.

She closed the door to her beautiful yellow room and leaned against it, her head down, tears stinging her eyes. She'd never be able to please Dad! Why even try?

Slowly she walked to the single bed and sank onto the edge of it. Her feet felt warm on the gold carpet. She picked up Munro, the

large furry white mouse that sat on her pillow
next to the large rag doll that Dara Cook
had given her. As she hugged Munro she
looked at the yellow walls and white furniture
with yellow trim. It was the most beautiful
bedroom in the whole world! Her artwork lay
on her desk. Maybe later she'd feel like
finishing her painting of the fox that Grandpa
had taken care of. Grandpa always doctored
sick and hurt animals, mostly wild animals.
When they were well, he'd turn them loose if
they were wild and find homes for them if
they were tame. Why wasn't she with Grandpa
right now instead of sitting here feeling bad
because Dad was mad at her for returning the
money to Mrs. Guthrie?

The bedroom door opened and Mom stuck
her head in. She smiled hesitantly. "I want to
talk to you, Teddy Jo."

"Come in, Mom." Teddy Jo's voice cracked
and she frowned. No way would she cry now!

Carol sat on the edge of the bed and slipped
her arm around Teddy Jo. Just a few months
ago Carol wouldn't have done that. She never
hugged or kissed Teddy Jo. She never talked to
Teddy Jo unless she had to, but now she was
a Christian and she and Teddy Jo had learned
to love each other.

Teddy Jo leaned her dark head against Mom.
Mom smelled like a rose and for once the
smell didn't sting Teddy Jo's nose.

"Teddy Jo, Dad doesn't understand why you

40

had to return the money, but I do. Be patient with Dad. He's better than he once was. Just a few weeks ago he'd have taken the money and kept it so that you couldn't have returned it. Once he learns that God loves him, he'll want to give his life to Jesus, and then he'll change just like I did."

"I know, Mom. I'll try harder, but he makes me feel terrible!"

Carol kissed Teddy Jo's cheek and Teddy Jo smiled. "Show me how you're doing with your reading."

Teddy Jo flushed and jumped up in agitation. She hated to read aloud. She was probably the only girl in the whole world in fifth grade who read at the third grade level! "Do I have to, Mom?"

"You're doing much better."

"I hate to read!"

"You'll like it as soon as you can read better, and the only way to read better is to practice. Get your book and sit down beside me and read a page."

Reluctantly Teddy Jo picked up her book from the corner of her desk and slowly walked back to the bed and sat down. Her heart beat so loud she was sure Mom could hear it. Her hands trembled as she found the page. She could paint for hours and hours, but if she had to read even one sentence, she'd freeze up and her brain would refuse to function.

Carol tapped the page. "Start right here."

Teddy Jo looked down at the page, then gasped in surprise. "That's a medallion! Mrs. Guthrie has one a lot like this. See the man with a skirt on playing the bagpipe?"

Carol nodded. "See this word, Teddy Jo? This word is *medallion*. Now you know the hardest word of the whole story. You can read it all. And see this word? It's *Scotland*, and this one is *bagpipe*."

Teddy Jo looked at the words and the picture of the medallion, and she laughed. It sure was funny to think that strange Mrs. Guthrie had helped with her reading. That was worth a whole lot more than the hundred dollar bill!

6. Marsha's Secret

"Teddy Jo, would you please read page forty-four." Mrs. Beeken crossed her slender legs and pulled her skirt over her knees.

Teddy Jo swallowed hard. Her hands were wet with perspiration as she looked at the page in her reading book. Someone laughed and someone else whispered and then more people laughed. Teddy Jo shot a look across the classroom. Marsha looked back at her with a smug look on her face. Teddy Jo wanted to sink out of sight. Marsha knew what a terrible time she had reading and Marsha was telling everyone around her. Teddy Jo bit the inside of her bottom lip to hold back the angry words that she wanted to hurl at the mean red-headed girl.

"Read, Teddy Jo," said Mrs. Beeken as she leaned forward in her chair. She sat with the reading group in a semicircle around her.

It was the lowest level reading group in the entire class, and Teddy Jo was embarrassed to be a part of it.

Teddy Jo blinked and focused on the page. Relief washed over her. It was the page about the medallion. She knew the words! She'd read this very page to Mom just Saturday. In a clear voice she read the page. She didn't stumble over a single word.

"Very good, Teddy Jo," said Mrs. Beeken with a nod of her blonde head. "Bobby, you read the next page."

With a smug look Teddy Jo turned her head. Her blue eyes bore into Marsha's eyes. Finally Marsha made a face and looked down at her desk. Teddy Jo laughed under her breath, then followed along with what Bobby was reading. He missed several words and she felt for him. Usually she read the worst in the whole group.

After reading group Teddy Jo walked to her seat with her head high and her book tightly in her hand. Her steps seemed loud in the quiet room.

"Medallion," whispered Marsha, wrinkling her nose.

Teddy Jo kept walking. She sank to her desk and glared at Marsha. Marsha's long red hair hung down her back. She wore a dark blue sweater with the collar of a lighter blue plaid blouse showing and new jeans.

With trembling hands Teddy Jo gripped the

edge of her seat. Her faded jeans felt hot on her legs and the neck of her sweater suddenly seemed too tight. Why couldn't Marsha leave her alone? Why was she always so mean to everyone?

The dismissal bell rang and Teddy Jo wanted to run to Marsha and punch her, but she forced herself to walk quietly to the hall for her coat. Noise erupted around her as she pulled her warm hat down over her ears. She tugged on her mittens as she walked around a group of people. She'd made plans to meet Paul just outside the front door, and then walk downtown to the variety store.

Marsha watched Teddy Jo push through the front door out into the cold winter day and anger rose in her. Just seeing Teddy Jo made her fighting mad and she didn't know why. She zipped her bright jacket as she ran toward the door. Teddy Jo thought she was so smart! Well, she wasn't! She was dumb and ugly and her hair was always tangled. And her grandpa was ugly, too. Marsha gasped as cold wind struck her. She was glad she didn't have a grandpa to play with her and take her to the park and everything. She sure didn't want an ugly old man doing things with her!

"Hey, Teddy Jo!" Marsha cupped her cold hands around her mouth and shouted above the other boys and girls.

Teddy Jo stopped and looked back with a

frown. She saw Marsha and then quickly turned and continued walking with Paul beside her.

Marsha pressed her lips tightly together and her cheeks flushed as red as her hair as she dashed after Teddy Jo. "Hey, Miller! How does a dumb girl like you know the word 'medallion'? Knowing it won't keep you from flunking fifth grade, you know!" Marsha laughed and looked around to see if anyone was laughing with her. Several girls were. But she knew if they knew her secret, they'd be laughing at her, too.

Teddy Jo wanted to stop and yell something mean back at Marsha, but she knew Jesus didn't want her to. She clutched Paul's arm and tugged him along at a run.

Paul stumbled and would've fallen, but Teddy Jo's grip tightened. The cold air hurt his lungs and he gasped and slowed and jerked free. "I don't want to run, Teddy Jo." He looked pounds heavier in his winter clothing. His nose was runny and his cheeks pink. "You don't have to run away from Marsha Wyman. She's taller than you but you're stronger."

"You know I don't fight anymore."

Paul rolled his eyes. Maybe one of these days he'd believe that and then he wouldn't be afraid of her.

A half block away, Marsha followed Teddy Jo and Paul with her hands stuck in her jacket pockets to keep them warm and her shoulders hunched to keep her neck and ears from freezing. She should just go home where it was warm, but right now she didn't feel like being alone. Maybe she'd have an adventure if she followed the Miller kids. It might be kind of nice to have a brother or sister. Maybe her mom would stay home more then, and maybe her dad wouldn't get angry and impatient as easily.

Just half a block from Main Street Marsha spotted a lone old woman carrying a bag over each arm. Marsha gasped and pressed her trembling hands to her suddenly hot cheeks. Teddy Jo and Paul were stopping to talk to Grace Guthrie! Why, oh, why had Grace Guthrie moved to Middle Lake? She should've stayed in Grand Rapids!

Marsha hid behind a tall maple tree and peeked around it. Several cars drove down the street. Boys and girls walked along the cracked sidewalk, shouting and laughing. An old man rode past on a bicycle, a cap pulled low over his ears and large gloves on his hands. Teddy Jo and Paul walked on and Grace Guthrie walked toward Marsha. She gasped and looked wildly around for a safer place to hide. Oh, she dare not let Grace Guthrie see her! Her heart raced painfully and all the color drained from her face.

"What're you doing, Marsha?" Cathy Norton stopped beside the tree and frowned at Marsha.

"I'm waiting for someone," said Marsha stiffly. She tossed back her hair. "But I'm not going to wait any longer. I'm going home right now."

"I'll walk with you. I'm going home, too." Cathy lived next door to Teddy Jo and they were friends. She sometimes was friends with Marsha, too. "Did you hear about Teddy Jo's hundred dollars?"

"What?" Marsha peeked over her shoulder, but Grace Guthrie was walking across the street so Marsha relaxed. "What about it?"

"Paul told my brother and he told me. Teddy Jo helped that funny bag lady and she gave Teddy Jo a hundred dollars." Cathy's blue eyes sparkled. Blonde hair peeked out of her warm knitted hat. She didn't think she'd part with that much money if she had it.

"Why would that . . . that woman give Teddy Jo a hundred dollars?" Marsha's skin pricked and excitement rose in her.

"Teddy Jo helped her find something, a necklace, I think, and she thought she was giving Teddy Jo a dollar. But, anyway, Teddy Jo returned the money. Isn't that funny? Did you think the bag lady would ever have that kind of money? My dad said she eats cat food because she doesn't have enough money."

"Cat food? That's not true!" It made Marsha sick just to think about it.

Cathy shrugged. She didn't know if it were

true or not, but she didn't want to fight about it. "Would you give back money if someone gave you that much?"

"I might. It depends." But she knew she wouldn't. She'd buy new clothes and a new soccer ball now that hers was scratched so badly. Then it would look better than Teddy Jo's.

They stopped at the curb and waited for a car to pass, then crossed the quiet street. Marsha looked back, but she couldn't see Grace Guthrie. She smiled. She was safe again.

"If *I* had a hundred dollars I'd buy a guitar," said Cathy. "I might take lessons."

Marsha tipped back her head and laughed. "You could never play a guitar! You have no coordination!"

Cathy flushed. "I do, too!"

"I'll bet you'll never be able to do anything. You'll end up being a bag lady just like Grace Guthrie!"

Cathy shook her head with a hurt look, then ran from Marsha to her house.

Marsha laughed and laughed. Then she stopped and tears pricked her eyes. Why had she done that to Cathy? Now she'd have to go home and be all alone until her parents got home. She shook her head. No! She'd turn around and go downtown and buy a candy bar. If Grace Guthrie was around she'd run around the block away from her.

She saw Grace two blocks from where she had been. Several boys and girls were yelling at her and laughing and making fun of her. Marsha quickly hid behind a parked car and listened and watched. She swallowed hard and doubled her fists as one boy grabbed one of the bags from the old lady.

"Give that back!" shouted Grace angrily. "You can't take my bag! You want me to call the police?"

"Maybe you should stuff a policeman inside your bag!" called a girl, and everyone laughed.

Just then Teddy Jo and Paul stopped beside Grace Guthrie. Teddy Jo glared at the boys and girls. "Leave her alone! And give her back that bag!" Teddy Jo lunged at the boy and grabbed the bag before he could stop her.

Paul stood by helplessly. He wanted to be a hero and do something really great, but his feet felt glued to the sidewalk.

Teddy Jo hooked the bag over Grace's thin arm. "We'll walk you part way home to make sure nobody bothers you."

"I can take care of myself!" Grace squared her shoulders and tugged her tattered coat tighter around her lean frame. "Them little kids don't bother me!"

Teddy Jo backed away and watched as Grace Guthrie walked stiffly out of the quiet crowd.

Paul touched Teddy Jo's arm. "Let's go home," he said just above a whisper. He didn't want to stay there and get beat up.

"Let's go," said Teddy Jo. She walked away with Paul close beside her. She heard someone call her a bad name, but she kept walking with her head high and her eyes sparkling.

6. Marsha's Secret

The howling wind blew large white snowflakes against the attic window. Marsha Wyman stood in the middle of the dusty floor and looked slowly around. Shivers of excitement ran up and down her spine. She rubbed her hands on her shirt sleeves. Dust tickled her nose and she rubbed it with the back of her hand. Would Mom and Dad get home from the café where they were having their Sunday morning coffee? Would they wonder why she was in the attic?

Slowly she walked to a large box and lifted the lid. Her stomach tightened as she stared down at the awkward-looking bagpipe that rightfully belonged to Grace Guthrie.

What would Teddy Jo say if she knew the truth? What would everyone in Middle Lake say?

Marsha wrapped her arms around herself

53

and moaned. Finally she knelt on the wooden floor and reached inside the box and lifted out a picture of Grandpa and Grandma Guthrie on their fifteenth wedding anniversary. How had the pretty woman with flaming red hair turned into the ugly bag lady of Middle Lake? Why didn't Mom do something to break the angry silence between them?

Marsha lifted out the bagpipe and it fell awkwardly over her arm. Someday she'd learn the whole story. She knew only that the bagpipe was involved. With a trembling hand she rubbed the mouthpiece, then blew into it. No sound came out. On TV she'd heard the wailing of the pipes and watched men dressed in kilts marching in a parade. Her ancestors had worn kilts and marched to the pipes across Scotland. Her Uncle Rob had played the pipes in a school in Grand Rapids, but he'd died in a car accident while he was still in high school and she couldn't remember him.

Grandma Grace Guthrie desperately wanted the bagpipe back. Marsha had heard her mother talk about it. Marsha's eyes narrowed. Just what would the old woman give in exchange for the bagpipe? Maybe the hundred dollar bill that Teddy Jo had returned?

A wicked light gleamed in Marsha's blue eyes and she hastily piled the bagpipe back in the box. She'd go visit Grace Guthrie and she'd make a deal with her!

Marsha's heart raced and she hesitated as

she looked at the photograph again. How would it feel to have a grandma who loved her, who did things with her? She shook her head and tightened her jaw. Well, she didn't have a grandma so she might as well not even think about such things!

Several minutes later she leaned her bike against the lavender house. Cold wind stung her skin. Snowflakes clung to her hat. She looked at the front door and waves of heat rolled over her. Oh, why had she dared to come here? She stuck out her chin and knocked loudly on the door.

Grace Guthrie flung wide the door, then gasped, and her face turned sickly gray. She wore a dark green bulky sweater and gray pants much too large for her slight body. Her small feet were pushed into a pair of men's leather slippers, scuffed and worn. "What do you want?" she asked in a strangled whisper.

Marsha forced herself to step inside before she could turn and bolt away down the deserted street. She looked around with a frown at the piles of boxes and magazines and odds and ends of furniture and junk. How could anyone live in such a place? With a nudge of her shoulder she pushed the door closed with a snap. The smell of coffee drifted around, almost covering up the musty, dusty smell of the room.

"Did Emily send you?" Grace pulled herself up and patted her thin gray hair in place.

"Mom doesn't know I'm here."

"Then why did you come?"

"You're my grandma!"

"I've been your grandma for eleven years and that never brought you before." Grace fingered the medallion around her neck. "Did you come to make fun of me and my house?"

Marsha tugged off her hat and unzipped her jacket. Oh, but she wanted to turn and run and not stop until she was safely in her home again. What would Mom do if she knew where she was right now? She'd left a note saying that she was out riding her bike. She looked right at Grace. The old woman was just a few inches taller than Marsha. "I came to make a deal with you, Grandma." She made the word *grandma* sound dirty.

"Did you, now?"

"I have something that you want." Marsha pulled off her jacket and stood with it over her arm. The room was almost too hot to breathe in.

"I've got to sit down. My legs aren't as strong as they used to be." Grace led the way to the kitchen, sank down on a padded chair, and leaned her clasped hands on the Formica table top.

Marsha's legs didn't feel very strong, either, and she gladly dropped to a chair across from Grace. The kitchen was warm and cozy, but very cluttered. Beans boiled in a pot on the stove. Marsha looked around to see if she could find any evidence of cat food. Finally she faced Grace. "I have something you want."

"So you said."

"It's true."

Grace leaned forward. "What's your name?"

Marsha swallowed hard. "Marsha."

"Yes, that's right. I'd forgotten for just a minute. And when did you find out that I'm your grandma?"

"When you moved into town."

"Why didn't you talk to me then or visit me?"

"You're a bag lady! Do you think I want anyone to know that the strange bag lady is my grandma?"

"Bag lady? I'm no bag lady."

"You carry bags around and collect things off the streets and out of people's garbage."

"I've got to live, don't I?" Grace clutched her medallion tighter. "Get on with the reason you came."

"I saw Teddy Jo Miller come in here last week. Did you tell her who you are?" Marsha locked her icy fingers together in her lap.

"She already knows who I am. Everyone does, it seems." Grace pushed back her chair, leaned back, and crossed her bony knees. The dangling slipper fell from her foot to show a heavy gray wool sock with a hole in the toe. "I didn't tell her about our relation, if that's what you're really asking."

Marsha breathed easier. Just then she

noticed the strange necklace around Grace's neck. She leaned forward and studied it thoughtfully. She'd seen something like that not long ago. Where had it been? Suddenly she remembered the reading book that Teddy Jo's group read from and the story about the medallion. So, that's how Teddy Jo knew the word! Oh, wouldn't she be curious if she wore the medallion to school?

"Why are you looking at my medallion that way?" asked Grace sharply as she clutched it with one wrinkled hand. "Did your mother send you here to steal my medallion just like she stole the bagpipe? Well, she can't have it! You go home and tell her I said that!" Grace jumped up and almost knocked over her chair. Angry sparks shot from her blue eyes and Marsha cringed back in fear.

"She didn't send me! She doesn't know I'm here!"

"Get on with what you want then!"

Marsha swallowed hard and fought against the fear that was enveloping her. "Do you want the bagpipe back?"

Grace gasped and seized Marsha by her shoulders. "Want it back? It's my one dream! Are you here to tease an old lady?"

"I'll trade the bagpipe for . . ." Marsha frowned in thought. Did she want the hundred dollar bill or did she want the medallion?

"Anything! Just name it!"

Marsha licked her lips and studied the medallion through narrowed eyes. "I'll take the medallion!"

Grace jumped back with a start and bumped into the stove. "Emily put you up to that, didn't she? Didn't she? She's wanted this ever since her father showed it to her when she was a little girl!"

Marsha walked around the table and stood with her hands on the back of a chair. She could hear Grace's raspy breathing. "I told you Mom doesn't know I'm here. And she won't know. Ever. I won't let her see the medallion."

"No!"

Marsha shrugged. "The bagpipe or the medallion. Maybe I could take it to a yard sale and sell it this spring."

Grace gasped. "Sell it? Sell it! No, no! You can't!"

Marsha flipped back her red hair. "I want the medallion, Grandma. I would keep it always." And wear it so that Teddy Jo could see it and wonder how she got it. "You want the bagpipe. Which do you want more?"

Grace bent over and groaned. "You've hurt me, girl. You've hurt me deeply. How can you make me choose? Both belong to me."

"But the bagpipe is in our attic tucked away in a box where you'll never see it or touch it. Think about that." Marsha watched Grace. The pathetic look tore at Marsha's heart and she had to look away. What was she doing? This woman was her grandmother! How could she be so cruel to her?

Finally Grace squared her thin shoulders and lifted her head proudly. "You bring me the bagpipe and I'll give you the medallion."

Marsha blinked in surprise. She had expected to be tossed out on her ear. "No. I'll take the medallion right now and I'll bring you the bagpipe as soon as I can do it without Mom knowing about it."

Grace walked to the sink and looked out the window above the sink and stared at the snow-covered backyard. Finally she turned back. Slowly she lifted the chain from around her neck and held it out to Marsha.

Marsha's hand shook as she reached for it. She slipped the chain over her head and the medallion hung almost to her waist. Tears pricked her eyes and she ducked her head and blinked them away. "I'll bring the pipes soon."

"Make sure that you do."

Marsha shivered at the cold tone of her grandmother's voice.

"If you don't have it to me before next Saturday, I'll spread the word around town that Emily Wyman is my daughter and that you're my granddaughter!" Grace jerked Marsha's jacket off the chair back and held it out to her. "Now, get out of my house!"

Marsha walked through the cluttered room to the front door. Cold air whipped against her as she stepped out of the lavender house. A strange yearning rose inside her. She wanted to turn and hand the medallion back and sit with Grace Guthrie and talk to her and be with her. But she couldn't. She wheeled her bike to the sidewalk and pedaled away, the medallion hidden safely inside her jacket.

7. The Medallion

Marsha sat on the edge of her bed looking thoughtfully at the medallion. She rubbed her finger around the gold rim and touched the man playing the bagpipe. The medallion was hers now. If she wanted, she could keep both the medallion and the bagpipe. What could Grace Guthrie do? She was too weak to break in and take it. Besides, she would never come within a block of the house. She wouldn't want to run into her own daughter.

Tears burned Marsha's eyes. How could a mother and daughter hate each other so much? Marsha pressed the medallion to her heart and stared fearfully across the green and gold bedroom that Mom had decorated just last year to make it a girl's room instead of a baby's. Someday would Mom get angry with her and kick her out and never speak to her again?

Someone knocked on her bedroom door and

Marsha jumped up, pulling off the medallion as quickly as she could. She stuffed it under her pillow and called, "Come in." She forced a smile as her mother walked in, wearing a winter coat and carrying a soft yellow scarf.

"You must start to school, Marsha. Why don't you have your coat on? Hurry up. I have a meeting to go to and I want you to be ready before I leave." Emily patted Marsha's flushed cheek and smiled. "After school we'll go do a little Christmas shopping. Time's getting away from us."

In the past few days Marsha had been so busy thinking about the medallion and trying to figure out a way to sneak the bagpipe from the attic that she'd forgotten about Christmas coming soon. She pulled her jacket from the closet full of pretty dresses that she very seldom wore. She liked jeans and shirts and sweaters better than dresses or skirts. But she couldn't convince her mother of that. "I'll see you right after school, Mom." This would be another day gone by without being able to get the bagpipe to Mrs. Guthrie. Would she really tell everyone that she was related to them?

"I must run, Marsha." Emily rushed away, leaving a trail of perfume.

Marsha waited until the front door slammed and then she pulled out the medallion and slipped it over her head. Quickly she zipped up her jacket, grabbed her hat and science book, and rushed out. Today she'd make sure that Teddy Jo saw the medallion. She'd make sure that Teddy Jo knew that she wasn't the only person around to get something from Grace Guthrie! But she would never, never let Teddy Jo know that Grace Guthrie was her grandma.

In school Marsha wore the medallion between her shirt and sweater so that she'd be sure that Teddy Jo saw it at just the right time.

The right time finally came just after school. Teddy Jo stood at the corner of the building waiting for Paul. Marsha knew she had to hurry home to go shopping with her mother, but she couldn't pass up the chance with Teddy Jo.

Marsha's blue eyes flashed mischievously as she tugged the chain until the medallion hung on the outside of her coat. "She'd have to be blind not to see this," muttered Marsha as she walked toward Teddy Jo.

Teddy Jo stood with her hands in her jacket pockets. Cold air nipped her nose and turned her cheeks red. She looked up to see if Paul was coming, but it was only Marsha, so she started to turn away. Today she didn't want to talk to Marsha. But she stopped midturn and stared in surprise at the medallion dangling against Marsha's coat. Teddy Jo's eyes widened. "How did you get that away from Mrs. Guthrie, Marsha?"

"This?" Marsha forced a light laugh as she

held up the medallion. "Is this what you're talking about, Teddy Jo?"

"That belongs to Mrs. Guthrie and she loves it! Did you steal it from her?"

"What a terrible thing to say! I don't steal. You might, but I don't. She gave it to me as a special gift. She wanted me to have it." Marsha tossed her head. "She said I could keep it forever."

Teddy Jo's heart turned over and she stepped closer to Marsha. "I don't believe you! I think you stole it from her. She wouldn't part with it and I know it!" Teddy Jo frowned thoughtfully. "Did you pretend to help her and then because she always pays her own way, ask her for the medallion? Did you do that, Marsha?"

Marsha forced a laugh through the lump in her throat. "She wanted me to have it. She likes me." Her stomach tightened and she suddenly wanted to run home and hide from everyone.

Teddy Jo shook her head. "No way!" She lunged at Marsha and knocked her to the ground and before Marsha could stop her, she pulled the chain off over Marsha's head, knocking off her hat.

Marsha rolled away and leaped up and looked wildly around for help. Others stood around watching, but none of them stepped forward to help.

Paul ran around the crowd and before he

could see what was happening, Teddy Jo grabbed his arm and pulled him quickly down the sidewalk.

Marsha doubled her fists and bit her bottom lip to keep from sobbing aloud with frustration. She wanted to run after Teddy Jo, but she had to get home to meet her mother.

Teddy Jo ran as fast as she dared with Paul. Finally she stopped and walked. "How could Marsha do it?"

Paul looked up at Teddy Jo, puffing hard. "Do what?"

"Look!" Teddy Jo held out the medallion. "Marsha stole it from Mrs. Guthrie! We're going to take it back to her right now!"

Paul tugged on his mitten until his thin wrist was covered against the cold. "Maybe she won't want to see us. Maybe we should keep it."

Teddy Jo stopped dead and glared at Paul and he hunched his shoulders and wished he'd kept his mouth shut. She finally walked away and he followed a few steps behind her.

Outside the lavender house Teddy Jo stopped and waited until Paul was beside her. She'd sure never admit it to him, but she was glad he was with her to go inside and face Mrs. Guthrie.

Paul rubbed his mittened hand across his nose and looked helplessly up at Teddy Jo. He never knew what to expect from her.

A car drove past on the street. A horn

honked from down the street. Somewhere nearby a baby cried. Teddy Jo shivered as she knocked on the lavender door. Maybe Mrs. Guthrie wasn't home.

The door opened and Teddy Jo gulped as Grace told them to come in.

"I thought you were someone else," said Grace with a frown. "But no matter. I don't have cookies today, but I could make toast."

Paul pushed past Teddy Jo to go to the kitchen, but she caught his arm and stopped him. He wanted to jerk away. He was hungry and she should know it.

"We can't stay, Mrs. Guthrie." Teddy Jo bit her bottom lip as she pulled the medallion from her pocket. "We brought this back to you."

Grace gasped, her face suddenly deathly white. "How did you get it?"

"From that mean Marsha Wyman! She dared to wear it to school today and she said you gave it to her. But I knew better. She's mean, and I know you'd never give her anything."

Grace held the cold medallion against her wrinkled cheek and tears sparkled in her tired blue eyes. "I'd like to keep it, Teddy Jo, but I want you to give it back to Marsha. I did give it to her. I want her to have it."

"No!" Teddy Jo shook her head and frowned. "I won't give it to her! It's yours!"

Grace caught Teddy Jo's hand and pressed

the medallion into it. "You take it right back to Marsha and do it now!"

"No!"

Grace turned to Paul. "Then you do it, Paul. You're a good boy and you won't argue with me."

Paul took the medallion and held it. It was heavy in his small hand. The chain slipped off the side of his hand and hung down almost to the floor. He didn't dare look at Teddy Jo or she'd make him give it back.

Teddy Jo breathed deeply, then almost choked from the bad smell of the room. "If we have to give it back, all right, but I don't like it one bit."

"I'll explain another day," said Grace crisply. "Now, take it and give it to her. Try to do it when she's alone. I don't want others knowing you stole it from her and brought it to me."

The words cut into Teddy Jo, but she lifted her head and pulled open the door. She wanted to grab the medallion from Paul and drop it on the floor and run away.

Paul stood uneasily on the sidewalk. He wanted to carry the medallion, but he didn't want Teddy Jo angry with him. Finally he held it out to her and she took it without a word and stuffed it into her pocket.

"I don't understand it, Paul," she said as they walked slowly down the sidewalk.

"Me, neither." He didn't know what he didn't understand.

"Why would Mrs. Guthrie want Marsha to have the medallion?"

Paul shrugged. He watched a squirrel run up a tree. The squirrel was probably going to eat a few nuts. *He* was hungry enough to eat nuts, shell and all.

"She loves her medallion."

Paul kicked a rock and it clattered down the sidewalk and onto a snow-covered lawn.

"Marsha must have forced her to give it to her."

For three hours Teddy Jo thought about the medallion as she watched out her front window for Marsha to get home. When the car finally stopped outside the garage, Teddy Jo grabbed her jacket and raced across the street before Marsha disappeared inside.

"Wait, Marsha!"

Marsha turned with a frown. Oh, but she wanted to knock Teddy Jo down hard! "What do you want?"

"She said to give it back to you," said Teddy Jo impatiently. "I don't want to, but she said I had to."

Marsha looked quickly at her mother, then waited until she walked inside. "Give it to me and don't ever say I stole it again!"

Reluctantly Teddy Jo held it out and Marsha snatched it and rammed it into her pocket before Mom saw it from the window. "What else did she say, Teddy Jo?"

"Nothing."

"I want to hear you say you're sorry."
Marsha stood with her hands on her hips and
her bottom lip thrust out.

Teddy Jo doubled her fists. "I'm not sorry!
I'd do it again if I could!" She turned and ran
to her house. Oh, but she hated Marsha
Wyman!

Teddy Jo stopped just inside the door.
Smells of fried chicken filled the air. The
corners of her mouth drooped. Jesus didn't
want her to hate anyone, not even Marsha
Wyman. But Teddy Jo lifted her chin defiantly.
She had every right to hate Marsha. Nobody
loved Marsha, except maybe her parents,
and she wouldn't, either! A band tightened
around her heart as she walked slowly to her
yellow and white bedroom.

8. Snowdrifts

The first day of Christmas vacation Teddy Jo ran to the window to see the lawn and walks piled with snow. Mom and Dad had had to stay home from work because of the snow. The news on TV said that stores were closed along with most businesses.

"I hate snow," said Linda as she stopped beside Teddy Jo to stare out the window. She'd made plans with friends, and now they couldn't go anywhere or do anything. She was stuck at home. What a boring, boring day.

"Let's go out and build a snowman," said Teddy Jo with a happy laugh. She would not let Linda's unhappy face make her feel sad. Today was a beautiful day! No school, and that meant no reading group! "We could build the biggest snowman in the whole world!"

"I'll help. I'll help!" Paul jumped up and down, then stopped when Larry walked in.

Paul ducked his head and sank to the corner of the couch and stared down at the beige carpet.

"I think I'd like to build a snowman, too." Larry stretched and yawned. "I'm glad we didn't have to go to work today." He pushed his plaid flannel shirt into his faded jeans. He looked happy and Teddy Jo stared at him, wondering if this man could be her father.

Paul held his breath and waited for Dad to click on the TV and bark at them to leave him alone in peace. Wouldn't it be nice to have a dad like Mike Brent's next door? Just maybe Grandpa was right. Maybe someday Dad would be a Christian and they'd be a happy family full of love. It made him tingle all over just thinking about it. He'd wrestle around with Dad and go places with him and tell him funny jokes just like Mike did with his dad.

Later the entire family stood in the snow in the front yard. Linda looked around with a frown. She didn't want to build a dumb snowman. She wanted to go shopping with her friends. Mom should've let her stay in her room and try on different makeup.

Paul scooped up a handful of snow and threw it at Teddy Jo. The ball splatted against her back and she turned with a shout, her eyes sparkling. Paul fell over into a snowdrift, laughing hard.

Larry picked up a handful of soft snow and rubbed it on Carol's face as she struggled and laughed and tried to push snow down his neck.

Laughter rang out from the Miller yard for the first time ever.

Teddy Jo stood very still and listened and marveled. Someday they would have a wonderful Christian family!

Several minutes later a tall snowman stood in the front yard. Teddy Jo wrapped her scarf around its neck and Linda found an old hat for its head. Linda laughed. It had been fun after all. Maybe she wasn't too old to play outdoors in the snow.

Teddy Jo picked up the snow shovel and pushed a heap of snow off the sidewalk. She looked up and down the street. Snowdrifts stood where the snowplow had pushed snow from the street. A few driveways were cleared and a few sidewalks. With a lot of work and time, she'd soon have their sidewalk cleared. Her dad was already at work on the drive so he'd be able to get the car out of the garage for work tomorrow.

Who would shovel Grace Guthrie's sidewalk? Would she have to walk through snowbanks in her old tennis shoes to get to the street?

Teddy Jo leaned against her shovel and frowned thoughtfully. Why should she even think about helping Mrs. Guthrie? Last time she tried to help, she had been hurt and embarrassed. So why try again? Maybe Mrs. Guthrie loved snowdrifts. Maybe she'd yell and tell her to stay away from her and her snowdrifts. Teddy Jo flushed and bent to the shovel and snow flew wildly until her arms felt heavy and weak.

"Hot cocoa for whoever wants it," called Carol from the front door. The smell drifted out the door, Teddy Jo sniffed it, and her stomach cramped with hunger.

She turned to walk to the house, but caught a movement in the window across the street. Had Marsha been watching her? Was she laughing at her because she'd had to return the medallion?

With a flushed face Teddy Jo ran into the warm house. She peeled off her snowy clothes and hung them on a hook in the laundry room. Snow scattered across the tiled floor as she pulled off her boots. She hooked her hair behind her ears, tugged down her red sweat shirt and walked to the kitchen to join her family for a cup of steaming cocoa.

Across the street Marsha walked away from the window and sat in front of the TV. Her mother was watching a soap opera and her dad was making fun of it. Marsha looked at them and opened her mouth to say something, hoping to gain their attention. But she snapped her mouth closed and leaned back in the corner of the large flowered chair. She touched the medallion that lay hidden between her shirt and pullover sweater. Her red hair was brushed neatly and clipped back with two blue barrettes. Finally last week, just after school on Wednesday, she'd been able to take the bagpipe to Grace Guthrie. The whole visit ran through her mind again.

"I was beginning to think I'd have to follow through with my threat," Grace said gruffly when she opened the door to Marsha.

Marsha stepped inside as shivers ran up and down her spine. "I couldn't get here before this."

"Well, you're here now." Grace looked at the box and tears filled her eyes and slowly slipped down her wrinkled cheeks. "Is that it?"

"Yes." Marsha blinked fast to keep back tears. Her throat closed over and she couldn't say anything. The medallion around her neck seemed to weigh more than a bag of sugar. For one wild minute she considered taking it off and returning it to the old woman.

Grace carried the box to the kitchen and Marsha followed close behind. Impatiently Grace pushed aside the clutter on the table and set the box down. She rubbed her eyes, pulled a tissue from the cuff of her heavy sweater, and noisily blew her nose. Her hands shook as she lifted the lid of the cardboard box. "Oh, I can't bear it!"

Marsha pulled off her jacket and sank to a chair. She felt sick to her stomach and the smell of cooked fish didn't help. Grace Guthrie's face brought more tears to her eyes. Oh, why had she started this? She should've stayed away from this old woman!

77

Grace lifted out the bagpipe and hugged it to her, laughing and crying. "Do you want to hear a bit of the pipes, Marsha?"

"Do you play?"

"I do. But not like your grandfather nor your Uncle Rob. Could they play! They could bring a tear to your eye and a lift to your heart."

Marsha locked her hands together and sat very still as she listened to the wailing music of the bagpipe that had been in her attic for years. It would be wonderful to know how to play. A great yearning started deep inside her but she forced it away. She couldn't learn. Who would teach her?

At last Grace lifted her head and smiled and the smile went right to Marsha's heart.

"Thank you for bringing it to me, Marsha. I didn't think I'd ever see it again."

"You paid to see it!" snapped Marsha.

Grace shook her head. "No, Marsha. I gave you the medallion to bring you back. Yes, I wanted the pipes." Grace touched them lovingly. "But I wanted you more. I hoped that you'd come see me and we could get to know each other. I'm tired of my loneliness. If Emily would take the first step, I'd forgive her fast enough."

"She'd be angry if she knew I gave you this. Or even that I talked to you."

"I know." Grace lovingly laid the bagpipe back in the box. "Maybe you should return it so you won't get in trouble."

Marsha shook her head hard. "No! You keep it. It's yours."

"All right. But I want you to come see me. I could teach you how to play it."

A smile tugged at Marsha's lips, but she refused to show it. Stiffly she stood up. "I'm leaving now. You've got what you want and I've got what I want."

Grace shook her head sadly. "No. I want more than this. I want a family. I want people to respect me and not call me the bag lady."

Marsha had grabbed her jacket and fled. When she reached home she'd locked herself in her room and sobbed until her throat ached.

She touched her throat now and swallowed hard. What was Grace Guthrie doing right now? Was she snowed in with nothing to eat? Did she have boots to keep her feet warm when she walked through the snow?

Marsha's parents laughed loudly on their way to the kitchen. Impatiently Marsha clicked off the TV, walked to the large picture window, and looked at the snowman the Miller family had made.

Just then Teddy Jo walked out of her house, picked up a snow shovel, and put it on her shoulder. Marsha jumped away from the window and bit her bottom lip. All of a sudden she wanted to run outdoors and talk to Teddy Jo and play in the snow with her. Marsha frowned. How could she feel that way? She must be sick. She didn't even like Teddy Jo!

Teddy Jo hummed a song that she'd learned in Sunday school as she started down the sidewalk.

The door opened and Larry stepped out. "Wait for me, Teddy Jo. I'll go with you and help you shovel Mrs. Guthrie's walk."

Teddy Jo gasped in surprise. Did she hear right?

"Paul's coming, too. He'll be right out." Larry picked up the snow shovel leaning against the garage and rested it on his shoulder. He wore a bright orange snowmobile suit that he wore ice fishing and heavy boots that reached to the calf of his leg.

Teddy Jo blew out her breath and shook her head. Wouldn't Mrs. Guthrie be surprised?

Paul slammed the door and ran to Teddy Jo's side. He carried the small shovel that Mom had bought him last week so he could help shovel snow. He felt ten feet tall as he walked with Teddy Jo and Dad down the street.

Many people waved and spoke to them as they walked to Lincoln Street. The sidewalk leading to the lavender house was packed with snow. Before long it was clear and the snow was piled high on either side of it.

The front door opened and Grace poked her head out. "What do you think you're doing?"

"Cleaning your walk," said Teddy Jo with a quick look at her dad to see if he was getting angry at Mrs. Guthrie's sharp tone. He didn't seem to be, and Teddy Jo breathed easier.

"I can't pay you!"

"We don't want pay," said Larry with a frown. "We just thought you needed to be dug out so you could get around easier."

"Well, so, you're done. You'd better get home out of the cold." Grace slammed the door shut.

Teddy Jo cleared her throat and twisted the shovel in her cold hands.

"So much for doing a good deed," said Larry sharply. "Let's go."

Teddy Jo followed Dad and Paul down Lincoln Street to Oak. She remembered something that Grandpa had told her.

"Teddy Jo, you help others because Jesus said to, not to get a kind word or a reward from them. Jesus said to love. No matter what anyone says to you, you do what Jesus wants. That is what's important."

Teddy Jo lifted her head and smiled. She'd helped Mrs. Guthrie and that's what was important. The old woman's sharp words wouldn't change what she'd done. She ran to catch up to Dad and Paul. "Thanks for helping me," she said with a wide smile.

9. Christmas

"This is for you, Teddy Bear Jo." Grandpa held out the gaily wrapped package and Teddy Jo took it with a cry of surprise and joy. He'd already given her a necklace, so she hadn't expected anything else.

She sank to the living room floor and tore at the paper. The rest of the family was already playing Space Invaders on the Atari set that Mom and Dad had bought the whole family.

Grandpa sat on the chair next to the tall Christmas tree he'd helped the family cut from his property. He crossed his arms and his navy blue suit jacket tightened on his broad shoulders. His striped tie hung loosely around his thick neck.

Teddy Jo's blue eyes sparkled with excitement as she saw the small suitcase. She tugged her yellow sweater over her new yellow dress pants and looked up questioningly. Did Grandpa think she needed a suitcase? She'd always used a small box or brown grocery bag to carry her clothes in.

"Look inside," said Grandpa, bobbing his shaggy eyebrows up and down.

She laughed and unsnapped it and lifted the lid. She gasped and sat very still. The case was full of art supplies. Oh, it was too good to be true! Never, ever did she dream of having so many pads of papers and pencils and paints and brushes! She lifted a few things out to find stretched canvas. Just a few days ago she'd wished for that very thing to paint the picture for art class. And here it was! She flung her arms around Grandpa and hugged him hard. Tears blurred her vision and she blinked them away. Her family wasn't interested in her art, but Grandpa was. He had told her often that she had talent. Someday she wanted to be a famous artist. "Thank you, Grandpa! Oh, thank you!"

He laughed and she felt the rumble of it against her chest. He smelled like after-shave lotion. "Someday you can tell everyone that your grandpa helped you with your career." He held her on his lap and stroked back her dark brown hair that she'd remembered to brush, as they talked about the picture she'd been working on for the school art fair.

Later, after the gifts were put away, Teddy Jo stood at the front window with Grandpa beside her.

"I like the snowman," he said. "I see the sun has melted it a little."

A door slammed and Larry's angry voice reached them. "I don't care what you say, Carol. I'm going ice fishing!"

"You promised to stay home all day long, Larry! You promised! You said you'd be here with the family all day long!"

"I changed my mind! I need fresh air! I need to get out of here." Another door slammed, then all was quiet.

Teddy Jo leaned her head against Grandpa's arm. "Why do they fight so much, Grandpa? Won't we ever be happy?"

"Don't be discouraged, Teddy Jo. Your dad has come a long way. One of these days he'll realize that God loves him, and then he'll want this family to be happy and be together. You said he helped you shovel Mrs. Guthrie's walk the other day."

Teddy Jo nodded.

"Just a few months ago he wouldn't have done that."

"I know." She sighed and gripped Grandpa's large hand. "I've wanted to talk to you about Mrs. Guthrie."

"What about her?"

"I feel sorry for her, Grandpa. She's so alone. But when I try to help her, she snaps at me."

"She doesn't know that you want only to be

her friend. She probably thinks you're nice to her for what you can get from her."

"But I'm not!"

"Pray for her and then do what you can for her. God can make her want to know more about you and your love. You can tell her that God loves her and wants to be her helper and friend."

"I wanted to take her a Christmas gift, but I was afraid to." Teddy Jo walked with Grandpa to the couch and sat down. Paul walked in and clicked on the TV. A football game blasted on and he quickly turned it down.

Grandpa rubbed his gray hair. "I think it would be very nice if you took her something. So what if she snaps at you? Does it make you any shorter or taller? No. It might hurt your feelings, but you can handle that." He smiled and winked, and she felt as if she could do anything.

"I'll go after a while. I think I'll take her a few oranges, too."

Across the street at Marsha's house, Marsha walked restlessly from the living room to the kitchen. Dad was watching the game on TV and Mom was reading a book on herbs that Dad had bought her for Christmas. Dinner smells still hung in the air. Absently Marsha picked up a piece of chocolate candy with a nut center and ate it.

What was Grace Guthrie doing today? Was she lonely?

Marsha frowned and bit back a moan. Would Grandma Guthrie grow older and older and die without her family around?

"No!" Marsha whispered with a hard shake of her red head. She would take Grandma the gift she'd wrapped for her! And she'd do it right now! "I'm going for a walk, Mom."

Emily looked up with a vacant stare, then nodded. "Be back before dark."

Marsha grabbed the small box from her room and hid it in the folds of her jacket as she ran to the back door. She pulled on her warm boots and wrapped her scarf around her neck. Excitement mixed with fear inside her. Part of her wanted to run fast to Grace Guthrie's house and part of her wanted to hide in her room.

She stopped just outdoors and breathed deeply of the crisp air. The bright sun glared on the snow and she blinked. Shivers ran up and down her spine. Dare she go see Grace Guthrie? What if someone saw her? What if someone learned the secret?

She hesitated, then lifted her chin high and ran down the sidewalk toward Lincoln Street. She reached the lavender house too quickly and she hung back, her eyes wide as she stared at the door. The box was awkward in her hand. Was she doing the right thing?

The door opened and Grace studied Marsha thoughtfully. "Did you come to see me, Marsha?"

Marsha licked her dry lips. "Yes. Merry Christmas."

"It is Christmas, isn't it?" Grace held the door wider. "Don't make me heat the whole outdoors. Come inside. I baked some cookies. Do you have time for a cookie?"

Slowly Marsha stepped inside. A white garland was draped from box to box. Silver icicles dangled prettily from the garland. The fragrance of freshly baked cookies almost blocked out the musty odor of old newspapers and magazines.

In the kitchen Marsha looked around at the furry red Christmas stocking hanging on the back door. A tiny artificial tree stood in the middle of the table. "I brought you a present."

Grace blinked in surprise. "You did?"

"Here!" Marsha thrust the box into Grace's hand.

Grace turned the box over and over. A tear slipped down and plopped on the back of her hand. She pulled off the red ribbon, carefully loosened the tape, and pulled the Christmas paper off. Her hands trembled and Marsha had to look away for a minute.

Finally Grace opened the box and looked inside. She gasped and dropped to a chair, her face white and her body shaking. "My medallion," she whispered. "My precious medallion!"

Marsha ducked her head and fought back the

tears that filled her eyes. Her gift had pleased her grandma.

Grace lovingly lifted the chain and hung it around her neck. The medallion settled in place on her shabby gray sweater. She patted it and rubbed it. "I never thought I would wear it again. Thank you, Marsha."

"You're welcome, Grandma."

Grace grew still and Marsha suddenly realized what she'd called this strange old woman. Marsha flushed.

"Well, I am your grandma. There's no big deal about calling me that when it's the way it should be." She jumped up and bustled about the kitchen, making tea and getting out a plate of chocolate cookies. "Did Emily see the medallion?"

"No."

"Does she know I have the bagpipe?" Grace motioned to it where it hung beside the old refrigerator.

"No." Marsha squirmed uncomfortably.

"Don't let her blame you when she does find out. You tell her I made you do it."

"I will." But Marsha knew she wouldn't.

Grace sat with a cup of tea in her hands and looked across the table at Marsha. "Merry Christmas, Granddaughter."

"Merry Christmas, Grandma."

Just then Teddy Jo knocked on the front door. Grace cocked her brow questioningly, then hurried to answer while Marsha stayed in the kitchen.

"Teddy Jo!"

Teddy Jo uncertainly held out the bag of fruit and candy that she'd put together special for Grace. "Merry Christmas."

Grace shook her head. "My, my. This is quite a surprise. Two gifts in one day. Thank you."

Teddy Jo stepped forward but Grace blocked her way. Just then Teddy Jo saw the medallion hanging around the old woman's neck. Marsha Wyman had given it back! What a surprise!

"I have company right now, Teddy Jo. You come back another day."

Teddy Jo walked away from the lavender house stunned. Maybe Marsha wasn't as mean as she'd thought.

10. Marsha to the Rescue

Once again Marsha stood outside the lavender house. Her heart raced and her palms were damp with perspiration. For the past five days she'd visited Grace Guthrie, and just last night she'd promised herself that she wouldn't come again. Mom would be very angry if she knew. The whole family would be disgraced if the people in Middle Lake learned the truth.

Marsha whimpered and turned away, then turned back. Being with her grandma just to talk to her and help her bake cookies was fun, too much fun to give up.

She looked quickly around before she knocked on the door. Grace didn't answer. Marsha knocked again, and again. Fear pricked her skin. What if Grandma had fallen and hurt herself? What if she'd died in the night the way Ned's grandma had died? Marsha thought of the boy in fifth grade who had come to school one day crying because his grandma was dead. He still cried when someone talked about grandparents.

Frantically Marsha knocked again, but still Grace didn't answer. With drooping shoulders Marsha walked away from the lavender house, wheeling her bike beside her. Street noises were background sounds to the worried thoughts that rushed through her mind. Gray clouds blocked out the sun. An occasional snowflake drifted through the air. Marsha looked straight ahead with large, haunted blue eyes.

A few minutes later she pedaled to Greer Park. Suddenly she stopped, almost tipping over. Grace Guthrie stood near the dumpster with her bags held protectively against her as several boys yelled at her, grabbing for her bags.

Anger rushed through Marsha and she pedaled quickly across the park. She leaped off her bike and it clattered to the ground. She ran at the nearest boy, ramming her fist into his stomach. He cried out as he fell down hard, grabbing his stomach.

"Get away from her!" cried Marsha angrily as she pushed between Grace and the boys.

"Look at the tough girl," said Jim Johnson with a sneer. He jabbed Marsha's arm with his fist and she cringed. "What makes you think we'll listen to you?"

"I can take care of myself, Marsha," said

Grace in a low voice. "Get away before you get hurt."

"I won't get hurt." She was tough all right. She hadn't become the best soccer player in the whole school without getting strong and mean. She stepped toward Jim Johnson with her eyes narrowed and her fists doubled. "Don't hit me again! Ever!"

"Oh, I'm scared! I'm scared!" Jim looked at his friends and laughed. They laughed with him.

Just then Teddy Jo, Paul, and Grandpa walked across the park.

"Having a little trouble here?" asked Grandpa as he stopped beside Marsha. He looked like a giant next to them.

The smile disappeared from Jim's face and he turned and ran away with the other boys close on his heels.

Teddy Jo stared in surprise at Marsha. Who would've thought that Marsha Wyman would help Grace Guthrie?

"Hello, Mrs. Guthrie." Grandpa stuck out his large hand. "I'm Ed Korman."

"I've seen you around," she said gruffly as she shook hands with him.

"I hope you're all right. Did the boys hurt you?"

"No. Marsha came to my rescue." Grace smiled proudly at Marsha.

Marsha's face flamed and she shrank away. She picked up her bike and pedaled away quickly. Tears of frustration filled her eyes and she blinked them away.

Teddy Jo watched her ride away and narrowed her eyes thoughtfully. Something was up, but what was it?

Grace moved restlessly. She'd scared Marsha off and she hadn't meant to do that.

"How about coming with us to have a cup of tea?" asked Grandpa.

Paul almost fell over in surprise. It would sure be funny to have the bag lady sitting in his kitchen.

"We still have Christmas cookies left," said Teddy Jo. "You'd like them." She didn't know if she wanted Grace to say yes or no.

Grace frowned down at her ragged tennis shoes. Could she go have tea with them, knowing that they lived right across the street from Emily? A slow smile crossed her face. That's just what she would do. Let Emily make of it what she would. "Yes, I'd like a hot cup of tea. It's colder out than I thought." She shifted her bags and walked beside Teddy Jo out of the park.

Grandpa talked with Grace all the way to 712 Oak Street. Teddy Jo listened to them and wondered if anyone was watching them and laughing at them because they were with the bag lady. She shrugged. What did it matter?

Marsha stood on her front porch and leaned against the pillar, then stiffened as she saw Grandma Guthrie with the Millers. What if

Mom drove in now? What would she do if she saw Grace Guthrie right here outside her house?

Grace saw Marsha out of the corner of her eye. Should she call Marsha over to go in with her? Would Marsha like that?

Paul opened the front door and stood aside for Grace to enter. He wrinkled his nose at her dirty smell.

Teddy Jo looked across the street at Marsha. Before she knew what she was saying, she called, "Hi, Marsha. Want to come over for a while?"

Marsha gasped. "Right now?"

"Yes. Mrs. Guthrie came to visit. Want to come, too?"

Marsha's stomach tightened and she chewed her bottom lip. Finally she ran down the steps and across the street. She didn't speak to Grace and Grace didn't speak to her.

Later they sat in the kitchen. Grandpa and Grace drank tea. Teddy Jo, Paul, and Marsha had hot chocolate that Teddy Jo had made. A plate of cookies sat in the middle of the table.

"You have a nice house," said Grace as she reached for another cookie. "You keep it nice and clean."

"We like living here," said Paul. "Once we lived in a worse house than your's."

Marsha glared at Paul and he sank back against his chair. What had made her mad at him?

Teddy Jo kicked Paul and he almost fell off his chair.

Grandpa quickly covered the awkward moment by talking about his woodworking shop.

Marsha moved restlessly. She wished she could talk as easily to Grace as Ed Korman. He didn't seem embarrassed to be with her at all. But then, she wasn't part of his family.

Finally Grace stood up. "Thank you for the tea and cookies, but I have to get on home."

Marsha jumped up. "I'll walk with you."

Grace shrugged. "If you want."

Teddy Jo told them good-bye and watched them walk out together. She tucked her tangled hair behind her ears. It was really funny to see Marsha and Mrs. Guthrie together.

"Mrs. Guthrie left her glove," said Paul, holding up a worn glove with a hole in the little finger of it.

Teddy Jo grabbed her jacket and slipped it on. "I'll take it to her." She grabbed the glove from Paul's hand and raced out, slamming the door behind her. Finally, half a block down Oak Street she caught up with them. They didn't hear her and she opened her mouth to speak, but Marsha was talking.

"I do want to come to your house if it's all right, Grandma."

"I want you to come if you want to come, Marsha."

Teddy Jo stopped dead. The bag lady was Marsha's grandma! The glove fell from her hand and landed on the toe of her boot. She leaned over, picked it up, and shouted, "Mrs. Guthrie, you forgot your glove!"

Grace and Marsha turned and waited, and Teddy Jo ran to them and handed the glove to Grace.

Without a word Teddy Jo ran back home. She knew a secret, a gigantic secret!

11. The Bagpipe

Marsha held the leather bag under her arm. The four sounding pipes rested on her shoulder. She blew into the blowpipe as she moved her fingers on the chanter as Grace had taught her.

"That's better, Marsha," said Grace, beaming with happiness. "You catch on fast. Three months now you've been practicing. Soon you'll be able to march down the street, playing the bagpipe like a pro!"

Marsha flushed with pleasure. It had been fun coming to visit Grace every day after school the past three months. It was hard to remember when she'd thought of Grace as the ugly bag lady. Maybe one of these days Mom would forgive Grandma, and Grandma would forgive Mom. And maybe Grandma would stop being the bag lady of Middle Lake!

Later, Marsha leaned her elbows on the

table and watched Grace fix tuna sandwiches, not cat-food tuna, but the people kind.

"Grandma, why do you dress the way you do?"

Grace looked down at her baggy shirt and worn black slacks. "I never thought one way or another about it."

"Have you always dressed this way?"

Grace stopped and lifted her head and narrowed her eyes thoughtfully. "You know, Marsha, I didn't. When your grandfather was alive, I always had nice clothes and kept a clean house. But when he died, things like that didn't matter. I moved here to be near Emily in case she ever wanted to give back the bagpipe, and things just slid along. My clothes wore out and I didn't want to spend money on more, so I wore what I found around town." She leaned against the table and studied Marsha. "Would it make you feel better if I looked different?"

Marsha flushed and grinned sheepishly. "Yes."

Grace pursed her lips. "I'll give that some thought, Marsha. Now, how about a sandwich?"

"Only half a one. I have to get home to eat with Mom and Dad. They don't care how long I'm gone after school as long as I'm home by six to eat."

"Don't they ask where you spend your time?"

"I just tell them I'm with a friend." Marsha

grinned and Grace winked. "I wish you and Mom would make up. I want to tell Mom and Dad that I can play the bagpipe."

"I'm too old and set in my ways, Marsha. I don't think I could make the first move. It's very hard for me to forgive Emily."

"What did she do to you? Why won't you tell me?" Marsha twisted her fingers until they hurt. She flipped her head to get her red hair out of her face. "You always say you'll tell me tomorrow."

"Maybe I won't tell you at all," snapped Grace. "You get yourself home and don't bother me any longer today."

"I might not ever come again!" Marsha grabbed her lightweight jacket off the back of the chair and ran around the table toward the door. "Who needs you? You're a mean bag lady! Mean!"

"Don't come knocking on my door, Marsha Wyman! I won't let you in!" Grace glared at Marsha.

Marsha tripped over a bag, caught herself on a box and ran out the front door into the windy March afternoon. Clumps of dirty snow lay in piles here and there against the homes along Lincoln Street. A dog barked and nipped at Marsha's bicycle tire. She yelled at it and almost tipped over as she jerked to get away.

She didn't need Grace Guthrie! She could get along without her just like Mom did!

At her home Marsha slammed the back

door, then stopped just inside the kitchen where Mom stood at the sink.

"What's wrong, Marsha?"

"Nothing."

Emily dried her hands and dropped the towel on the counter beside the sink. "Marsha, I've looked all over for the Easter baskets that I always decorate and set around the house. Do you know where they are?"

Marsha shook her head and started to walk past to go to her room and pout.

"Maybe they're in the attic. Your father might have put them there even though I told him not to. I'll go look."

Marsha's head shot up and her eyes widened in alarm. "No! No, Mom! I'll look. I don't mind at all."

"Well, if you're sure."

"I'm very sure!" Marsha practically ran to the stairs and up to the attic. She clicked on the light and looked around at the dusty boxes and old furniture. My, but that had been a close call! Mom must never learn that Grandma had the bagpipe.

Marsha searched behind things and under things, but she couldn't find the wicker baskets that Mom wanted.

Emily walked in and Marsha almost tumbled over.

"I can't find them, Mom. Let's go eat. I'm hungry."

"Your dad's not home yet." Emily walked

slowly around the attic. "I haven't been up here in ages. It's so dirty! I really will have to come up and clean one of these days."

"I'll clean, Mom!" Marsha's heart raced in alarm. "I'll have fun doing it."

"No, Marsha. You can help me, but I couldn't let you do it alone. It's a dirty job." Emily walked toward the spot where she'd kept the bagpipe and Marsha's heart skipped a beat. "There are a lot of old memories up here. Some good and some bad."

Marsha tugged at Emily's arm. "Let's get out of here! It's dusty and I'm going to sneeze."

"Not yet, Marsha. You go on down if you want. I want to look at something first." Emily walked around, then turned to Marsha with a frown. "Something is missing."

Marsha looked as innocent as a baby. "Oh?"

Emily shifted around a few boxes, moving one and then another. "I can't find the box that holds the bagpipe."

Marsha backed to the door. Her legs felt hot inside her jeans.

Emily muttered to herself as she continued to look. Suddenly she jerked up and her face reddened with anger. "The bagpipe is gone! It's gone! Where is it?"

Marsha shook her head. She couldn't speak around the hard lump in her throat.

"Do you have it in your room, Marsha?"

She shook her head.

"Did my mother come in here when I wasn't

home and take it?" Emily's voice rose shrilly.

Marsha again shook her head. She leaned weakly against the door.

Emily stabbed her fingers through her light brown hair. "I know Fred wouldn't take it. So where is it? Momma must have it!"

Marsha wanted to run, but she couldn't move. A car honked outdoors. A floorboard creaked.

Emily stepped forward. She gripped Marsha's arm. "I see that guilty look on your face, Marsha. Tell me what you did with the bagpipe and tell me now!"

Marsha swallowed hard. She looked down at the dusty floor and groaned. She tried to pull free, but Emily's grip tightened.

Emily caught Marsha by the arms and shook her hard. "You tell me what you did with my bagpipe! Tell me *now!*"

Marsha jerked up her head as anger washed over her. "I gave it to Grandma! I carried it to her house and gave it to her!"

Emily stumbled back, her hand clutching at her throat. "Get away from me, Marsha. Get away from me before I do something that I'll regret later!"

Marsha turned and ran down the stairs, snatching her coat as she raced out the back door. She grabbed her bike and pedaled away, tears streaming down her flushed cheeks.

12. New Clothes

Grace walked thoughtfully to her bedroom and looked in the door mirror. Was that old dowdy lady really her? Had she lived in such a daze that she hadn't realized what was happening to her? She did need new clothes! And she needed a bath.

In the bathroom she filled the tub with hot water and steam blurred the mirror. Slowly she slipped down into the sudsy water and soaked until she was wrinkled. She washed her hair with shampoo that smelled like strawberries. Carefully she clipped her toenails and fingernails, then rubbed lotion all over herself. With a frown she looked at her clothes. Finally she slipped on clean things that were worn and ragged. She really did need new clothes! The stores were open late tonight, so she'd walk right downtown and shop. Wouldn't Marsha be surprised?

But would Marsha ever come back?

Grace sighed as she tied her old tennis shoes. She was a mean old woman without the ability to forgive others. Teddy Jo knew about forgiving. She should take a lesson from Teddy Jo.

Grace rummaged through her cupboard until she found the hundred dollar bill that she'd accidently given Teddy Jo last fall. In another cup she found more money, then stood with a frown while she tried to remember where she'd put another hundred dollar bill. Frantically she searched the cupboard. Perspiration dotted her face. Finally she remembered that she'd slipped it between the mattress and box spring of her bed.

At last she was ready to walk out the door. She looked at the two bags that she always carried and she shook her head. Today she wouldn't take them. Today she wasn't going to pick anyone's garbage.

Chilly wind whipped her long coat around her thin legs as she walked down Lincoln Street. Just as she walked past a pink house on Oak Street Anna Sloan walked out, carrying her purse and wearing a beautiful all-weather gray tweed coat.

"Hello, Mrs. Guthrie." Anna smiled as she pulled her car keys out of her purse.

"Hello, Mrs. Sloan. It's a beautiful day, isn't it?"

"Very. Are you going downtown?"

"Yes."

"I'm on my way. Would you like a ride?"

Grace hesitated. Anna Sloan didn't seem to be embarrassed to be seen with the likes of her. "Thanks. That would be nice." It had been a long time since she'd been in a car. She'd sold hers years ago.

In the car Grace leaned back with a smile. Her life was in for one great change after another. The car smelled of leather and perfume. "Mrs. Sloan, do you have any grandchildren?"

"Yes, one granddaughter named Kandy. She lives just outside of Port Huron so I don't get to see her as often as I'd like." Anna stopped at a stop sign and smiled at Grace. "Do you have grandchildren?"

Grace hid a smile. If only she could tell Anna the truth! "Yes. One." She turned to look out the window. "I just wish I could be with her more, but I had a fight with my daughter and we're not speaking." Grace snapped her mouth closed. She'd never told anyone that, at least not a woman who was almost a stranger.

"That's too bad. A family is important. God created the family and Satan has been trying to tear it apart since the beginning of time."

"I believe that." Grace moved restlessly. "I know it's mostly my fault for my family being apart, but I have a hard time forgiving my daughter."

Anna pulled into a parking place outside of

Penney's. "I'm sorry, Mrs. Guthrie. I know that God can help you forgive. He loves you and he loves your family. He wants his very best for you."

Grace nodded. She knew that, but she'd forgotten it somehow. She smiled at Anna. "Thanks for the ride and the nice words. I'm going to buy myself some new clothes."

"I'm sure you must be excited about it."

"You wouldn't care to help me, would you?"

Anna smiled and nodded. "I'd love to!"

"I've been out of touch and I don't know just what's in style."

Anna laughed gaily and Grace liked the sound of it. "Mrs. Guthrie, we are going to have fun!"

"Call me Grace."

"And I'm Anna."

In Penney's the clerk stared openly at Grace, but she ignored the rude stare. She and Anna looked through the racks of clothes and selected several outfits. Anna showed her a pair of dress slacks and blouse that would look nice on her. The price tag almost choked Grace, but she carried the new underclothes and slacks and blouses into the changing room and slipped into new clothes. She stared at the slender woman and shook her head. Could that really be the same woman as the one in her mirror at home?

While Grace was in the fitting room, Anna surveyed a row of dresses. She found a simple, but attractive shirtwaist. "Grace, here's a dress to try on," said Anna, handing the dress through the partition.

Grace looked at it and finally slipped it on. She hadn't worn a dress in almost five years. She shook her head in disbelief. This was not the bag lady of Middle Lake! She'd have to get it!

Grace eyed herself in the mirror for several minutes, then changed back into a slacks set she felt more comfortable in. Before she paid for the items she asked the clerk to clip off the price tags on the navy slacks and flowered blouse she was wearing.

At the shoe department she slipped on flat-heeled shoes. The panty hose she wore felt strange, but the shoes felt stranger still. Anna handed her a pair of two-inch heels and she laughed and tried them on. Suddenly she felt years younger. She stood up and teetered back and forth.

"I don't think I can handle these," she said.

"You'll learn to walk in them," said Anna with a laugh. "They'll look beautiful with your dress."

"All right." Grace carried the two pairs of shoes to the counter. Now all she needed was a new coat.

It was already dark out as Grace walked outdoors with Anna beside her. She caught a glimpse of her reflection with Anna and it looked like two well-dressed women out on the town. She laughed. "Nobody will recognize me now."

"You look wonderful, Grace! How about having a bite to eat with me? My treat."

Signs along the street blinked off and on. People walked along and not one of them poked fun at Grace or laughed at her and called her the bag lady. "I'll be glad to go out to eat. I haven't been since James died."

"Tonight is a celebration."

"It is, Anna. I am not the town bag lady any longer. I am Grace Guthrie!"

"You are a valuable woman, Grace. God loves you."

Tears pricked Grace's eyes. "That's good to know." She'd think more about that when she was alone.

Much later Anna dropped Grace off in front of the lavender house. Grace said thank you, then carried her bundles to the front door. It was hard to find her keys in her new purse, but finally she did. Before she could slip the key in the lock a hand gripped her arm.

"What are you doing at my grandma's house? Get away from here! She's not home!" Marsha shivered. She'd been waiting outside the door for a long, long time and she was cold and hungry.

Grace smiled. The streetlight didn't light up the sidewalk very much, but even if it had, she knew Marsha wouldn't have recognized her. "When will Grace Guthrie be home?"

110

Marsha looked closer at the woman. The voice was very familiar. "Do I know you?"

"Do you, Marsha?" Grace chuckled, then sobered. "What are you doing here alone this time of night? Why aren't you home where you belong?"

Marsha backed away, suddenly frightened. "Who are you?"

"Enough games, Marsha. I'm your grandma. I'm all dressed up like a person should be."

"Grandma?" Marsha's mouth dropped open and she stared at the well-dressed woman in the nice-looking coat and slacks and shoes. "Grandma?"

"Yes." Grace unlocked the door and opened it and clicked on the light. "Now, you tell me what's going on." She saw Marsha's red eyes and pinched look around her nose. "What happened to you, Marsha?"

Marsha sniffed, then burst into tears. "Oh, Grandma! I ran away from home! I'm going to live with you forever!"

13. A Family Reunited

Grace held Marsha's hand tightly as they walked down the sidewalk. Streetlights cast an eerie glow. A TV blared from a house they passed. "Marsha, you've told me what happened with your mother. Don't worry about me. I can handle Emily. She has no business being angry with you for something that's my fault."

Marsha stopped and turned her face up to Grace. "Grandma, please, I want our family to be together and be happy. Teddy Jo's grandpa always does things with Teddy Jo. He's at her house a lot and they're so happy. Can it be that way with us? Do you have to keep on fighting with Mom?"

"It's hard for me to forgive and forget, Marsha."

"But could you try? Please?" Tears sparkled in Marsha's eyes.

Grace sniffed and nodded. "All right. I'll try." In her heart she prayed, "God if you really love me like Anna said, and if you can really help me forgive like Teddy Jo said, then help me now!"

Marsha stopped just outside her door. Shivers ran up and down her back. "I'm scared, Grandma."

"What? A Scot scared? Never!"

Marsha laughed shakily. "Let's go inside."

"I'm ready when you are." Grace gripped her new purse tighter. Emily was going to be very surprised.

Marsha opened the door and the light streamed out with the smell of coffee. No sooner had she stepped inside than her parents rushed at her.

"Marsha! Where have you been? We've been so worried!" Emily grabbed Marsha and hugged her close.

"We were ready to call the police," said Fred as he hugged Emily and Marsha together.

Grace stood quietly beside the door and watched her family. She looked around the tidy kitchen and suddenly realized how messy her house had become. It would take much longer to clean her house than it had to change her image!

Marsha finally pulled away from her parents and turned to Grace. "Mom, we came to talk, Grandma and I did."

"Grace Guthrie?" asked Fred in surprise.

114

He lifted his dark brows and his mouth fell open.

"Momma? Momma, is that you?" Emily stared at Grace in bewilderment. "You look the way you used to look before Papa died."

"It took Marsha's love to bring me back." Grace squeezed Marsha's hand.

Emily stepped forward and her face suddenly darkened with anger. "You! You made my own daughter steal from me! How could you?"

"Don't, Mom," said Marsha in anguish. "Please, don't!"

Fred caught Emily's arm and pulled her back against himself. "It's time we got this whole thing settled. Let's go in the living room and sit down and talk like mature adults. Emily? Grace?"

Emily sniffed and tossed her head.

Grace's jaw tightened, but she nodded.

Marsha walked with Grace to the living room and sat beside her on the couch. An icy band tightened around Marsha's heart. She locked her hands together in her lap. Her red hair was mussed and her eyes still pink from crying.

Emily sat on the edge of her chair and Fred perched on the arm of it with his arm protectively around her. She swallowed hard. "All right, Mother. I want to know if you're going to bring back the bagpipe that you had Marsha steal for you."

Grace's head shot up and her eyes blazed. "It's my bagpipe! It belonged to my precious

115

Rob and before that to his father and his grandfather. How can you call it stealing when it is mine!"

"Rob wanted me to have it. So did Papa. And you know it." Emily jumped up in agitation. "This isn't getting us anywhere. I'm too upset to deal with this."

Grace pushed herself up. "You're upset? I've had to live with this heartache for nine years now! I lost both my children at once, one by a car wreck and the other because of deliberate murder!"

Marsha gasped.

"Now, Grace," said Fred.

"I did not murder Rob! I've told you over and over. It was an accident! He wanted to take the car. He wanted to drive himself! I know I should have since the roads were icy, but I let him go and I've had to live with that, but I didn't murder him!" Emily burst into tears and Fred pulled her back to her chair and held her close.

Grace sank to the couch and Marsha caught her shaking hand and held it tightly.

"Please, Grandma," whispered Marsha tearfully. "Don't blame Mom any longer."

Grace leaned back and closed her eyes. Without God's help she couldn't forgive and forget. Teddy Jo had said that he helped her forgive, so surely he would help in such a desperate situation as this. She cleared her throat and leaned forward. When Emily's sobs subsided Grace said, "Emily, I will forgive you and forget what has passed." As Grace spoke the words, a great burden lifted inside her and she was able to smile. "I want you to forgive me for this separation and for the anger between us. We are a family and I don't want to be apart from you a minute longer."

Emily chewed her bottom lip. She looked up at Fred and he nodded. She sniffed and studied Grace thoughtfully.

"Please, Mom," said Marsha in a soft voice. "I want Grandma to be a part of this family. I love her." Marsha peeked at Grace and smiled shyly. "I do love you, Grandma."

Grace blinked back tears. "And I love you, Marsha."

"I never expected to see this day," said Emily brokenly. "Momma, I will forgive and try to forget. I have missed you so much! And I hated to see Marsha without a grandma. Now, what will we do about the bagpipe?"

Grace squared her shoulders. "I'll keep it, of course."

Emily sighed loud and long. "Then what is settled, Mother? I want the bagpipe. You have the medallion and I want the bagpipe."

"No!" Grace shook her gray head. "No! I won't part with it again! You can't ask me to!"

"Why can't we settle the matter of the ownership of the bagpipe another time?" said Fred as he rubbed his long fingers through his dark hair. "We have cleared the air about

Rob. That's a start. You two are sitting in the same room and talking. That's a start. We'll leave the matter of the bagpipe until another day."

Emily swallowed hard and finally nodded.

Slowly Grace opened her new purse and rummaged inside. She lifted out the medallion and held it out to Emily. "I have had this for years. I want you and Marsha to have it now. Is that a fair trade?"

Marsha watched the medallion twist and turn on the end of the heavy chain. "But Grandma, you always wear that! You love it!"

Grace bit her bottom lip. "There comes a time when you have to decide what's more important, people or possessions. I love my medallion and I love my bagpipe, but I love you, Emily, and you, Marsha, and yes, you Fred, more. For years I've lived out of kilter because of my grief. But Marsha and that little Miller girl across the street helped put me back in place. I feel as if I'm in my right mind for the first time in years. It's not just this outward appearance that has changed, but I've changed on the inside, and I'm even going to change my house by cleaning out all the junk that I've collected since I moved here." Grace took a deep breath and her eyes misted with tears. "Emily, if the bagpipe means so much to you, then you can have it. I taught Marsha to play, so she'll be able to play it and it won't just sit in the attic out of sight."

118

"Momma! Are you really giving it to me willingly?"

"Yes."

"I'll bring it over often and play it for you," said Marsha.

Grace nodded. "You do that, Marsha. I'll like that a lot."

"What about the medallion?" asked Fred as he held it up and studied the Scotsman on it.

"I'm giving them both to Emily," said Grace in a voice just above a whisper.

Emily burst into tears and knelt at her mother's feet and sobbed with her head in her lap. Grace rubbed Emily's soft hair and whispered words of love to her.

Marsha watched her mother and her grandmother together and she smiled through her tears. Their family was together at long last.

At eleven o'clock they drove Grace home. She stood beside the car outside the lavender house and looked at Emily. "I'll bring the bagpipe out to you if you'll wait just a minute."

Emily nodded.

Slowly Grace walked inside the house and lifted the bagpipe from the wall. "Good-bye, my friend," she whispered. She laid it in the box that Marsha had brought it in and slowly carried it outdoors to the waiting Emily. Cool wind blew her new coat around her thin legs. The box felt heavy in her hands.

Emily stood beside the car. She looked inside the box at the bagpipe. Slowly she took the medallion from Fred and hung it around Grace's neck. She touched the box with the bagpipe. "Momma, I want, we want you to keep both things. Someday Marsha and I will have them, but while you're still with us, we want you to keep them both and enjoy them."

"And I'll keep coming for lessons," said Marsha.

Grace held the box to her. The medallion dangled on the outside of her coat. "Thank you, Emily."

Emily kissed her mother's wrinkled cheek. "I'll see you tomorrow."

"Tomorrow," whispered Marsha from the backseat of the car.

Grace nodded and turned and walked into the lavender house with the bagpipe and the medallion and the deep love of her family.

14. Easter

Teddy Jo stared at the school clock, wishing it would move faster so school would be out and Easter vacation would start. Maybe if the clock moved fast enough she wouldn't have to have reading group today. Sharpening her pencil would take up some of the time. She tucked her tangled hair behind her ears, picked up her stubby red pencil, and walked to the sharpener. As she twisted the handle, her pencil grew even shorter.

"I know something you don't know," whispered Marsha.

Teddy Jo looked over her shoulder to find Marsha standing in line, waiting with a pencil in her hand. "What do you know?" She would not get mad at Marsha!

"Grace Guthrie is my grandma!" Marsha waited for the surprised reaction, but Teddy Jo only shrugged.

"I've known for a long time."

"And you didn't tell anyone even when you got mad at me?"

Teddy Jo ducked her head sheepishly. "I wanted to, but I knew it wasn't right to do. I knew you wanted to keep it a secret."

Marsha's mouth dropped open, then she snapped it shut. "Well, it's not a secret any longer!"

"Good. She's not a bag lady any longer, either. I saw her yesterday and I didn't even know who she was until she told me."

Just then Mrs. Beeken frowned back at them. "Teddy Jo, it is time for reading. Will you bring your book and hurry?"

Teddy Jo flushed painfully as she picked up her book and walked to her group.

Mrs. Beeken wrote a word on the board and Teddy Jo sank lower and lower in her chair. She was supposed to know the word, but she'd forgotten all about it.

From back in the classroom Marsha said, "That's an easy word, Mrs. Beeken. Everyone knows it's 'automatically.' "

"Marsha!" Mrs. Beeken frowned at her.

Teddy Jo looked over her shoulder and studied Marsha thoughtfully. Marsha grinned at her and suddenly Teddy Jo knew that Marsha had done it just so she'd know the new word. Teddy Jo smiled and turned back to the reading group. She knew almost all of the words now that Marsha had told her the hardest one.

After school Teddy Jo pushed her way outdoors into the warm sunlight to find Marsha to thank her, but she wasn't in sight. Paul ran up to her and pulled at her arm.

"Guess who I just saw!"

"Who?"

Paul's eyes grew big and round in his small face. "Mrs. Guthrie! And she is not ragged or anything! And she didn't have her bags and she wasn't digging in the dumpster!"

"Where is she now?" Teddy Jo looked around and then spotted Grace on the sidewalk in front of the school. "Let's go talk to her." Teddy Jo caught Paul's hand and pulled him in a fast run. His little legs pumped up and down as he tried to keep up with her.

Grace turned and saw them. "Hello, kids. Have you seen Marsha?"

"She's already gone," said Teddy Jo.

"You're not a bag lady," said Paul in awe.

Grace laughed. "Not anymore. And my house is all cleaned out, too. Anna and your grandpa helped me clean it out. It's spic-and-span now." She squeezed Teddy Jo's thin shoulder. "I wanted to thank you for helping me last fall when I needed help. You started the change in me."

"I did?" Teddy Jo's heart swelled with pride.

"Come over this afternoon if you can and

listen to Marsha play the bagpipe." Grace
touched the medallion that hung around her
neck and rested against her flowered blouse.

Teddy Jo hesitated.

Paul moved restlessly. "I want to come hear
her play."

Teddy Jo smiled and nodded. "Me, too."

Several minutes later Teddy Jo and Paul sat
in the living room of Grace's house and
listened as Marsha played the bagpipe. Teddy
Jo looked around in amazement. She hadn't
known Grace had a living room. It had been
piled high with junk. To her surprise she
learned that the house had a living room, two
bedrooms, a kitchen and a large bathroom
big enough to hold a washer and dryer. Now
the house was clean and tidy.

Marsha wiped off the blowpipe and held the
awkward instrument out to Teddy Jo. "Do you
want to try it?"

"Oh, yes!" Teddy Jo took it and listened as
Marsha told her what to do. A strange noise
came out and Teddy Jo laughed.

Paul's hands itched to get ahold of the
bagpipe and try it out. He laughed so hard at
the sounds Teddy Jo made that he almost
fell off the sofa. Finally it was his turn and with
plenty of help, he made a weird sound that
wasn't close to being music, but he swelled up
with pride. He could play a bagpipe. He sure
could!

Teddy Jo wished she could take the bagpipe

home with her and play it for her family. She knew she couldn't, but she told them about it and even Dad said he'd go visit Grace with them someday and listen.

"We could go over tomorrow morning," said Larry as he clicked on the TV.

Teddy Jo looked quickly at Mom. "But tomorrow is Easter. We're going to church. All of us are."

"Not me," said Larry with a shake of his head.

"But you promised, Larry," said Carol.

"Did I?"

"Yes, you did, and so did Linda," said Teddy Jo firmly.

"Our whole family is going," said Paul. "I got new pants to wear. And shoes."

Larry scratched his head. "Well, if I promised, then I guess I'll have to go."

Teddy Jo's heart leaped. Since she'd become a Christian she'd gone to church with Grandpa every Sunday. Grandpa had said that one day the whole family would go to church together. Finally it was happening, even if it was only for Easter Sunday. Someday Dad would enjoy going as much as she and Paul and Mom liked to go.

Sunday morning the Millers drove out of their drive just as Grace Guthrie walked inside the Wymans' house.

Marsha ran to her. "Happy Easter, Grandma!" She stopped short. "You're all dressed up! You're wearing a dress! I've never seen you wear a dress."

Grace laughed. "And I've never seen you wear one. You run in and change. We're all going to church this morning. We have so much to be thankful for; I thought it would be nice to go as a family."

Emily heard from the doorway and she nodded. "You're right, Mother."

"What church should we go to?" asked Fred. "None of us are much into church going."

Grace laughed softly. "I know just where to go."

"Where, Grandma?"

"We'll follow the Millers. I know where they go and that's where we'll go. That family has something special."

Marsha thought of the times Teddy Jo could've done something to her and didn't. She knew it was because Teddy Jo was a Christian. Maybe she could find out what to do to become a Christian by going to Teddy Jo's church. "Yes, let's go to that church, Dad."

"All right. I'll give everyone ten minutes."

In fifteen minutes they were in the car, driving to church on Easter Sunday.

In the large church auditorium Teddy Jo sat between Linda and Grandpa. Paul sat on the other side of Anna and Mom and Dad sat beside Paul. The whole pew was taken up by their family. It seemed very strange, but nice. She touched the soft folds of her dress. Two yellow barrettes held back her hair that was brushed neatly for once. She turned her head and her eyes widened in surprise as the Wyman family and Grace Guthrie walked in and sat down across the aisle. She nudged Grandpa and whispered, "Look!"

He turned his head and smiled, then leaned down to Teddy Jo. "It's all because of you, Teddy Jo. Your life touched them and they'll never be the same."

Teddy Jo sat up straighter and squared her shoulders. God's love in her had helped work a miracle! The miracle wouldn't stop now, but would continue until Grace and her family were Christians.

Marsha looked around with interest. So this was what church looked like inside. Maybe it wouldn't be so bad to come all the time.

Grace leaned against the soft padding in the pew and listened as the organ played. A peace settled over her and she smiled. She patted Emily's knee. It was good to be together again.

Teddy Jo stood with everyone and sang the Easter songs, proclaiming that Jesus was no longer dead, but alive. From the corner of her eye she peeked at her family. Even Dad was singing. Joy rose inside her and she sang louder with her head up and her blue eyes sparkling.

ABOUT THE AUTHOR

Hilda Stahl was born and raised in the Nebraska Sandhills. When she was a young teen she realized she needed a personal relationship with God, so she accepted Christ into her life. She attended a Bible college where she met her husband, Norman. They and their seven children now live in Michigan.

When Hilda was a young mother with three children, she saw an ad in a magazine for a correspondence course in writing. She took the test, passed it, and soon fell in love with being a writer. She would write whenever she had free time, and she eventually began to sell what she wrote.

Hilda now has books with Tyndale House Publishers (the Elizabeth Gail series, The Tina series, The Teddy Jo series, and the Tyler Twins series), Accent Books (the Wren House mystery series), Bethel Publishing (the Amber Ainslie detective series, and *Gently Touch Sheela Jenkins*, a book for adults on child abuse), and Crossway Books (the Super JAM series for boys and *Sadie Rose and the Daring Escape*, for which she won the 1989 Angel Award). Hilda also has had hundreds of short stories published and has written a radio script for the Children's Bible Hour.

Some of Hilda's books have been translated into foreign languages, including Dutch, Chinese, and Hebrew. And when her first Elizabeth Gail book, *The Mystery at the Johnson Farm*, was made into a movie in 1989, it was a real dream come true for Hilda. She wants her books and their message of God's love and power to reach and help people all over the world. Hilda's writing centers on the truth that no matter what we may experience or face in life, Christ is always the answer.

Hilda speaks on writing at schools and organizations, and she is an instructor for the Institute of Children's Literature. She continues to write, teach, and speak—but mostly to write, because that is what she feels God has called her to do.